RENTED ROOMS

RENTED ROOMS

a collection of short fiction

Linda A. Lavid

iUniverse, Inc.
New York Lincoln Shanghai

Rented Rooms
a collection of short fiction

All Rights Reserved © 2003 by Linda A. Lavid

No part of this book may be reproduced or transmitted in any form or by any means, graphic, electronic, or mechanical, including photocopying, recording, taping, or by any information storage retrieval system, without the written permission of the publisher.

iUniverse, Inc.

For information address:
iUniverse, Inc.
2021 Pine Lake Road, Suite 100
Lincoln, NE 68512
www.iuniverse.com

ISBN: 0-595-27183-9

Printed in the United States of America

To the Kirsch boys, Peter and Miles

Contents

High Wire	1
Kindred Spirits	6
The Accident	10
Luck	28
The License Plate	32
EE O NAA	40
Casper's Quarry	53
Ka-ching	66
Birth From a Star	71
Shadow Man	78
The Smuggler	88
Moose	93
Elsie's Disappearance	107
A Father's Love	111
Aunt Leona	117
A Hero Among Us	127

High Wire

With a towel around his waist, T.J. opens the bathroom door of the motel room, walks out and pivots to the mirror. "Aren't you getting up?" he says to the air around him.

I see the back of him, his wide shoulders, narrow torso. The slight sheen of wetness glistens between his sharp shoulder blades that rise and ripple under his skin. He lifts an arm and runs his fingers through his sandy-colored hair, tweeded with gray. In his reflected image, he juts out his chin and turns his face slowly, passing his fingers along his taut jaw line. He appraises himself with hooded, sleepy eyes, vaguely reminiscent of James Dean, all edge and adolescence.

From the mirror, he gives me a dry, uninspiring glance. "You taking the afternoon off?"

"No," I say. "I got another ten minutes. Got here late, remember?"

He nods, steps around the bed and collects his clothes, bobbing for socks, underwear. He then walks to the chair, and lets the towel fall. The back of his long lean body is exposed: solid, compact. He bends over and slips up his boxers.

My point of interest strays to the flocked wallpaper that's mildewed and curling from the walls. Could someone be spying on us from a hole in the wall? They say it happens. I squint and look for a discreetly-placed blackened lens behind the many spots (mold, blood?) that could be harboring the peeping Tom's camera, and his prying, darting irises. I lie very still and listen for a video camera, its groan and whir…. But there is none.

We must seem like a married couple (and we are of course, just not to each other) to whomever is leering behind the wall since we have the habit of having sex under the covers. No photo-shoot opportunity here. Not that it was always like this. We had our moments ensconced in his office when he'd call me in just before closing.

Could I take a short letter? "Sure," I had said, sitting up straight, legs crossed, with a pad and pencil propped on one knee, my ear keenly attuned to the sounds of an emptying office: the slam of drawers, the clicks and ceasing drone of computers, copy machines being turned off for the night.

We'd stay seated, not saying a word as people flitted by, with an occasional "See you tomorrow", "Have a nice evening". His staring watery eyes bored into me as he waved them off. Within moments, beams of headlights from cars exiting the parking lot would arc across the room. "Light in your eyes?" he'd say rhetorically as he turned and drew the blinds. He'd then get up, walk around his desk and quietly close the door. The click of the latch echoed loudly in the cleared silent office, providing the stimulus to my Pavlovian response. Breathlessness and moans would quickly follow.

He now asks. "Did you make arrangements for the hotel in Chicago next week?"

"Yeah, the Sheraton."

He sits, rolls up one sock, inserts his toe, and pulls it to his knee in one fluid motion.

Wes, my husband, dresses differently, not only what he wears, but in the order he puts them on: jeans first, socks afterwards. But this shouldn't be surprising, we all have our way of doing things.

T.J. groans. "I can't believe I have to spend an entire Saturday with that idiot from R and D."

"Oh, big Dick's not so bad. Just make sure he's fed."

"Easy for you to say."

"What do you mean?" I say with some resistance.

T.J. sits back, his knees jut out to the sides. "The guy's a slug. Can't do anything for himself. Pompous ass. You don't know the half of it. Such a big shot. Sends me to get the coffee, like I'm some gopher. Hell, I'm the one making all the deals. He's just there for backup, to answer the odd question. It's me that gets them to sign up."

The company we work for sells edible desserts made from chemicals and obscure vegetable byproducts. We've cornered the market and cater to those individuals who can't tolerate milk or wheat or eggs which are, as some studies show, 70 percent of the world population. And that's a lot of people, not to mention a lot of eclairs.

I lift my head, punch the pillow and settle back in.

T.J. shakes his head. "You're going to be late."

"Cover for me," I tell him, half wanting to see his reaction, test his loyalty; after all isn't that what lovers are supposed to do?

"You're on your own. Got a meeting at three in Batavia. Won't be going back to the office."

I scan his smooth relaxed face. Could he be lying? Of course he could. It's what goes on between us: lies, secrets, fabrications of where we are, who we're with, what we're doing. But isn't that part of the excitement–standing on uncertain ground, not knowing.

This is what I do know. He's been married for thirteen years to a rather tall, angular, unnaturally blond-haired woman named Maureen who works in a bank and wears severe manlike suits and who, when calling the office leaves brief laconic messages, rarely requesting to speak to her husband directly.

He loves his wife, so he says, it's just that she doesn't understand him. I've interpreted this to mean certain things in the hieroglyphics of man-speak; specifically that she doesn't perform the way he'd like her to perform, which most likely involves some aberrations from the norm, that is to say any sexual act that is not procreative by form, function or design.

In any event he loves his wife, as I love my husband.

How to sum up Wes? All American, I'd say. Preoccupied with the lawn, having a spotless car and checking the weather channel at every click of the remote. Not that there's anything wrong with that, but let's face it, it's a never-ending battle; something you can never get your arms around; something that is never quite resolved.

T.J. carefully judges the ends of his tie. The ideal knot comes out the best when one loose end is measured to the length of his fingertips. He makes an adjustment. "How's this look?"

"A little longer," I say.

If Wes wore ties, he'd knot them his own way and wouldn't be asking me for directions. I like that T.J. consults me. Although I have to say, if he did it often enough, I'd probably want him to figure things out for himself.

He slips the knot to his neck. "So do you want to meet next week?"

Do I? I smile vaguely. His tentativeness makes me think. When do affairs end? And how? Are they supposed to go out with accusations, slamming doors; or simply dry up, like a shallow creek bed in late summer?

"On Wednesday? Same place, same time?" I ask.

He reaches for his jacket. "Of course."

"I'll have to check my schedule."

A perplexing look clouds his uncomplicated face. "Your schedule? What's to check? You get an hour lunch."

Our eyes make contact through the mirror, distantly and removed.

He scratches the back of his neck. "Well, if that's how you want to leave it."

My mind wanders in cool detachment. I'm wavering on a high wire in the middle of nowhere with only one place to go, and it's down fifty feet.

The motel door slams shut, leaving me alone and chilled. Two men, such luxury. But I don't have two men, not whole ones, that is.

They're mostly just pieces, spare parts, exchanged, fitted, to meet certain needs, basic and otherwise. What spare part do I bring to the equation? I look at the sparkled ceiling and wonder. Glitter, fairy dust?

※   ※   ※

Author's Note:

What is a short story? For me, it's a piece of work that hovers around a quintessential moment, an event or occurrence that happens and changes the character, an epiphany. Distill life to those certain moments, and voilá, you got yourself a tour de force, however petite.

Initially this story began with the last paragraph. I thought it was powerful, but my dear friends were instantly confused. In my vague recollection of a TV show, I recall a contestant taking blocks of words and putting them in some salient order. Writing fiction is a lot like that. In finishing this story, I learned that abstractions are best presented at the end.

Content. A woman has an affair. My first mental image of her was as a young girl soaring downhill on a bicycle. Her feet were off the pedals, her hair, a long mane, flew behind her. She was a girl addicted to the rush. Perhaps that's what led her to have an affair.

In this rendition of cheating spouses, the bloom is off the proverbial rose. The final romp ends with a whimper and the girl who lives for the rush discovers the illusion of love is fragile.

"High Wire" was first published in Wilmington Blues.

Kindred Spirits

Veronica never worked a day in her life. Why bother? Her job was to look good and be a man's lucky charm. She had been blessed with thoroughbred legs, and eyes the color and depth of Carribean waters at dusk. As time went on, her looks only got better, like a fine bronze statue whose velvet patina went beyond art to something timeless, unforgettable.

It was a heavy load to bear, being such a constant source of attention, but Veronica handled it well, for the most part. She smiled demurely, spoke breathlessly, and swept into a room as if she were carried on the broad wings of a phoenix. So, what problems could a woman like this possibly have? Like any fine photograph, what one saw was only part of the reality.

Veronica, beneath the beauty, was a murderer, cool and calculating. And while this did not cause her any problems either morally or materially, it sometimes got in the way of her love life. Trips to the Bahamas or Paris had to be put on hold if she were in the middle of "an act of reprisal". Yes, Veronica was a vigilante, a cause she embraced after her three-year-old niece was snatched from her bed by a gas meter man. Her niece's body was never found, but his was—nicely tucked inside a steamer trunk and char-broiled.

Her recent engagement had taken her to a hick town outside of Chicago where people looked unwell, possibly from too many chili dogs. There she rooted for a joker named Viper who belonged to a moronic motorcycle gang unimaginatively named, Blacksnake.

Viper had been accused of skinning his girlfriend alive. Apparently, he had wanted his potatoes fried, not mashed. The incident made national headlines and after a quick call to the dead woman's mother, Veronica was activated.

Unfortunately for Viper, he was out on bail, and as he fiddled around with carburetor problems in his backyard, he got tangled up in the cross hairs of Veronica's scope. After she pulled the trigger, dismantled her AR-180, and casually descended a rooftop one hundred yards away, she visited Nieman Marcus in the city. There she found the most darling black suit, snug and short. The only problem that remained was what to tell Jonathan, the man she presently loved.

She had been seeing Jonathan for six months. Together they made a formidable couple, both tall, slender, with faces on the verge of aloofness and vulnerability, a most curious combination. Jonathan had approached her in the stairwell of their apartment building. Did she know where the closest laundromat was? And on a Thursday morning, her usual time to wash, he appeared. First, they shared some bleach, then a coffee, and soon thereafter a candle-lit dinner.

On her drive back home from Chicago, she punched in his cell number. "Hey, baby."

"Wuz up doll?"

"Sorry I had to cancel the movie on Thursday."

"No problem."

"What you been up to?" she asked.

"Missin' you. How's your aunt doin'?"

Veronica didn't like lying, but she couldn't very well tell him the truth. "Much better."

"How sick was she?"

His question unnerved her. Was there an underlying trace of suspicion? "Another false alarm. It was gas, not her heart."

"You must feel relieved."

"Yes, very."

A silence hung in the air. She waited for him to say more but nothing came. She picked up the slack. "Dinner tonight?"

"Are you sure you can make it?"

There was sarcasm in his tone. Was he getting jealous? She glanced at the car clock. "I should be home in two hours. I'll make that shrimp dish you like."

"Okay, but let's make it around eight. I got some errands to run."

"Great. Love you."

"Love you more."

🍁   🍁   🍁

After a luxurious bath, Veronica slipped into lace underwear and a satin robe. By the time Jonathan knocked on the door, a fire was burning and mellow saxophone riffs filled the room.

His kiss was deep and long.

"Maybe I should visit my aunt more often," she said breathlessly.

His boyish grin melted her weak and before she had a chance to pour some wine, he scooped her in his arms and carried her into the bedroom.

The following morning, as Jonathan showered, Veronica cleaned up the bedroom. She stacked the dirty dishes, made the bed, and picked up clothes. While hanging his sport coat, a folded page fell to the floor. It was a map of metropolitan Chicago. She smiled. Certainly, it had to be a coincidence. Still, she rifled through the jacket. Tucked neatly inside the patch pocket was a receipt for a motel in the town where Viper lived. Her eyes zeroed in on the date—yesterday. She reeled in disbelief. Had he followed her? Was he an undercover cop? Or most alarming, did he have a bullet with her name on it? Veronica bolted into survival mode and dove across the room. Digging deep into her underwear drawer, she grabbed a snubbie.

Ten minutes later, Veronica sat across from Jonathan at the kitchen table. The Sunday Times was splayed between them.

After a sip of coffee, Veronica casually asked, "So what did you do while I was away?"

His eyes never left the newspaper. "Nothing much."

"Go anywhere?"

"Nope."

Veronica reached into her robe pocket and felt the comforting hardness of metal. "Why are you lying to me?"

With no response, he folded the paper, scribbled some words, then tossed it to her.

Her eyes scanned an article: *Akron man accused of vehicular manslaughter of six teenagers is acquitted.* Beneath he had written: *Ohio is pretty this time of year. Shall we drum up some business?*

Veronica hoped her shock was barely noticeable. She then looked deep into his eyes and saw a kindred spirit. "Yes, let's."

❧   ❧   ❧

Author's note:

Years ago a woman in Germany took a gun into a courtroom and shot the man who had raped and killed her daughter. The callousness of perpetrators juxtaposed to the helplessness of victims is heartbreaking. I like this story immensely. Retribution gives me great satisfaction without having to serve time.

Veronica is enigmatically beautiful—tall, thin and flawless. Quite by accident, I learned a lesson: in using descriptions such as Carribean waters at dusk, velvet patina, broad wings of the phoenix, her essence suddenly took on epic proportions. Writing is in the detail, and the more unique, the better.

"Kindred Spirits" was first published in PLOTS WITH GUNS!.

The Accident

Katya sits, unfazed, on their overstuffed couch, while Lew slams the kitchen cupboard doors, one after another, loudly, deliberately.

He's trying to get her attention, she imagines, waiting for her to scurry in and ask "what's wrong", but she isn't going to nibble, not after thirty-seven years of marriage, not after being a fish on a hook once too often.

Closing her eyes, Katya imagines standing on a sunny beach at the water's edge with tiny waves nipping at her toes. Suddenly, a clamor of metal erupts. Katya jolts upright and looks toward the kitchen. He must have pulled the silverware drawer out too far. After a few moments, she hears the singular clink of odd pieces of flatware being returned to their molded spots. Well, Katya thinks, that should keep him quiet for a while. She settles back into the sofa and closes her eyes again.

Her two o'clock appointment had phoned yesterday calling on a line with static and background traffic noise. He seemed in a rush, asking if he could come around in the morning, at eight, if you can imagine that! He even tried to bribe her with muffins. What was it about men, always trying to arrange you into their schedules?

"Kay!" Lew yells out.

Katya opens her eyes. "Yes dear."

"Where's the damn sugar?"

Sugar. So that's what all this clatter is about. The measly sugar which she never uses. And swearing besides.

"Kay, did you hear me?"

After an unhurried pause, she answers. "On the counter, near the pot."

Lew lumbers into the living room in his retirement clothes, looking like a repairman. He's wearing a dark-blue utility shirt and pants set, of which he has six, one for every day of the week except Sunday. It's a self-assigned uniform for the fledgling business he started four months ago. Blue Man Maintenance and Cleaning is what the ad reads in the Penny Saver—not that he gets very many calls, but just in case, he's ready from Monday through Saturday for any job, none too small.

"That's the first place I looked," he tells his wife. "It's not there."

"Maybe you took the bowl into the garage, and stop calling me Kay. I'm Katya, especially when people are over."

His gaze darts around the room. "What people?"

Katya ignores him. "I have a reading in five minutes," she tells him. "I need to study."

Her husband pats his chest pockets, then feels his legs. What's he looking for—his car keys? Is he about to leave?

That was the only problem with having strangers visit their home. She never knew if she'd need protection.

Lew turns away. "A half hour. That's it, Kay. I have to finish up on the Noonan's garage."

"Katya. It's Katya," she reminds him.

He waves his hand as if he's heard enough and trudges into the kitchen.

Katya watches him leave. She hates his uniform. The lackluster blue drains his face making him look paler and grayer than he should, and tired too. How many times has she suggested something different to wear? She's even bought him several golf shirts in the chalky colors of after-dinner mints; the kind of shirts that make you think of summer. But he's put them away unworn, still tagged, and she isn't going to argue.

She reaches for her business cards and pulls one out. The red block letters read: KATYA—HAND READER.

She admires her name—KATYA, mysterious yet tasteful, and so much better than boring "Kay". It sounds gypsy, not that she's ever known one. But she can imagine a dark-haired woman dancing in the night around a crackling fire, the flames casting light and shadows around her spinning form. KATYA, a woman with chains of gold around her neck and wrists and ankles, who seduces the swarthy men with her curling hands and body turns. Of course, Kay is nothing of the sort. Not at fifty-eight, not with anemic frizzy hair that's falling out in clumps. She sighs deeply and glances around the living room.

Everything is in order. Swatches of tapestry dress the sofa arms. Odd scarves—some lace, others translucent—veil the lamps and shroud the table tops. A line of smoke from the sparkler-stick incense snakes up in the corner and fills the room with a sweet thick haze.

She checks herself in the panel mirror one last time. The long coral top hangs loosely from her shoulders skimming her breasts and nicely avoiding the contact of any bulges below. Its matching skirt, thick with tiny pleats, touches the floor. Nothing these days is short enough for her five-foot frame. Still, there are advantages. She doesn't need to bother with stockings, just an old pair of slide-on slippers will do.

She then goes into the kitchen to put on a pot of tea, a welcoming gesture.

🍁   🍁   🍁

Lew, hunched at the kitchen table, sips his coffee.

"So you found the sugar," she says.

He shifts a glance at her. "No."

"Well, if you can't find the bowl, why not just get more from the bag."

He turns and peers out the window.

She really doesn't have the time for this but she marches over to the cupboard and while on tippy-toe, surveys the shelves. She moves the flour, honey, the bottles of oil and vinegar from one side to another. "Oh," she says, "I guess we're out."

"No kidding."

Katya shuts the cupboard door and decides, again, not to give it another thought.

She grabs the kettle and fills it with tap water. Then she remembers—the sugar bowl is on the sideboard, in the dining room with the tea cups. She had put it there the night before for her visit today. But Lew is almost finished with his coffee and it hardly seems the best time to let him know. Have him steep with the tea, she decides, and she turns on the burner.

Lew straightens up in his chair. "Someone's coming."

Katya sidles up behind him, lightly resting her hand on his shoulder and stoops down to get a better look.

The car, white and glimmering, has a rack on top. It enters the driveway slowly.

"What kind of car is that?" Katya asks Lew.

"Volvo."

"Expensive?"

"Yep. Full of air bags too."

The car stops. After a moment, the door opens. A young man gets out. He's a young girl's dream—blue-black hair, thick and longish that tapers over his collar. He's wearing a dark-brown leather jacket with khaki pants.

The man squints into the sun, then slips off his coat and puts it back into the car through the driver's window. Eyeing the house, he strolls toward it.

"You get the door." Katya says and she rushes from the kitchen not waiting for a response.

From the other side of the wall, Katya hears a knocking, then the skid of Lew's chair and his slow heavy step. The deadbolt clicks, the door creaks open.

"I'm looking for Katya," the young man says. "Is this the right place?"

"The one and only," Lew says. "Come in. I'm Mr. Katya."

Finally Lew says her name, but hardly in the way she expects.

"I'm Austin."

"Pleased to meet you. My wife…"

Katya considers this her cue. Standing as tall as possible, she makes an entrance. The man turns.

He's even more handsome close up. His light blue shirt, buttoned down at the collar, is ironed. Knifelike creases run down his arms to the folded-back cuffs. He has an olive coloring that glows.

Katya extends both her hands and wraps them around the hand he offers. His grip is solid and warm; his skin, supple and smooth. College educated, most likely, with a clean job, she assumes, in an office where there are no temperature extremes, and with a girlfriend or mother or wife who does the dishes.

She lets go of his hand.

"I'm making some tea," she says. "It should only take a minute, then we'll begin."

"Fine," he says, smiling with teeth as even and white as piano keys.

Katya can't ever remember seeing a man so perfect, except for maybe Cary Grant. But he was in the movies, not live and in color right in her kitchen. She brushes a few strands of hair away from her face and peeks down at her feet, fearing her bare stubby toes might be poking out.

"Beautiful day for a ride," Lew says.

"For sure."

"So how was the drive?"

"No problem. Thruway was clear."

"Coming from Buffalo?"

"Yeah."

Lew leans against the counter and folds his arms. "That should've taken about an hour and a half."

Austin glances at his watch. "A little under, maybe."

The kettle whistles. "Excuse me," Katya says as she patters between the two men. She turns off the gas.

"Yep, they finally finished that construction after the exit," Lew says. "Bridge work. Took'em two years. You're lucky you missed that."

"Mmm," Austin agrees.

Katya stretches, reaching for the teapot in the cupboard above.

"Here, let me get that for you," she hears the young man say as he comes up close behind.

His hand lightly touches the small of her back while his extended arm rises beside hers. It's almost like they're dancing, ballet dancing and for a moment she thinks of leaning back, feigning a fall to see if he'd catch her. Such a notion!

Instead she withdraws her arm and turns slightly. "Thank you."

He smiles again, a broad-faced smile, not just with his mouth but with his eyes, glimmering and dark. He hands her the pot.

"You happy with the Volvo?" Lew says. "I hear they can be expensive to fix."

Austin steps away from her. "I haven't had any problems so far."

"Lucky for you. Tuneups alone can run close to a hundred and fifty."

"Let's see," Katya says loudly, "I have regular tea, of course, but maybe you'd like some herbal—"

"Aren't those the cars that have electrical problems?" Lew interrupts.

"Excuse me, dear, but I was asking the nice man about what kind of tea he'd like," and she pulls out a drawer lined with colorful boxes. "There's rose hips, chamomile, lemon zing, sass—"

"Maybe he'd like coffee." Lew cuts in again. "Men don't drink, what'd you call it…lemon zing?"

Katya wants to shake her husband, send him to his room, do whatever it takes to stop him from being his usual bad-humored, rude self.

She takes a deep breath and focuses on Austin. "Would you prefer coffee?" she asks evenly.

Austin's eyes flit between the couple. "Regular tea sounds fine. Thank you. Thank you both."

Katya grips the handle of the pot and steadies the hot side with a padded glove. Turning toward Austin, she asks, "Shall we get started?"

"Sure," Austin says.

Katya pivots around and advances toward the living room.

"It's nice meeting you," she overhears Austin saying to Lew. As Katya leans her shoulder into the kitchen door, the young man rushes over, reaches around her and pushes the door open. Such a gentleman, she thinks, so refreshing, so pleasant.

Katya slips through the doorway. "By the way," she calls back to Lew, "the sugar's on the buffet."

🍁   🍁   🍁

Like most of the homes in the area, their living room faced the water. Where other towns had a small square and monument right smack in the center, Susquadaga had its lake.

Austin brushes past her. "What a great view!"

She agrees.

The mid-afternoon sun is casting a honey glow on the town. Small white houses, much like theirs, run along the curving road that winds around the water. And trees, hundreds of them, some pine, some still bare from the winter, gather in clumps, rising and falling with the rolling hills. The lake, slate gray and still, without a ripple or wave, seems so peaceful. And the ducks are back, sailing over and around the water, up and down and turning, and for a moment it feels as if she and the young man are cradled in spring.

Katya nods to the chair that faces the window. "You can sit here," and she puts the pot down on the table. "I'll get the cups." She steps over to the dining room where she stops for a moment and contemplates the tea cups. She decides on the only two that match—the Royal Albert pair with roses. Perfect for her nicely-mannered man. The cups rattle as she makes her way back to the table and eases into her seat.

"Can I pour you some tea?" she asks.

"Yes, but allow me," he says.

Katya can't remember the last time someone actually did something for her without having to ask. She sits back in her chair and watches as he does the honors. He has a natural upward curl to his lips that makes him seem everlastingly serene, and she can only remember children as having such long feathery lashes. Sunlight caresses her back, warming her inside and out, and for the first time in months, she feels toasty.

"Shall I get the cream and sugar?" Katya says, wanting to be useful.

"Well, not for me."

Kayta flutters. Already they have something in common.

She reaches out across the table. "Let's begin with your left hand."

Austin nests his curled hand into hers. Gently she strokes his palm. With each sweep, his warm dry hand opens wider.

"You see," she begins to say, "your hands are like road maps, with lines and mounts and valleys..." And she tells him about the gypsies and the planets and the elements. She presses and pokes, first feeling his left hand, then his right. The more she speaks, the more she forgets about how odd she looks, or how old, or fat. She even forgets about her husband.

❦   ❦   ❦

Lew stands at the kitchen table with his hands in his pockets, looking blankly out the back window. He had summed up Austin the minute he saw him—a know-it-all-pretty-boy-rich kid, who never worked an honest day in his life. No coke ovens, or orange dust up his ass, that was for sure. Lew's seen plenty like him, the president's son, the vice-president's nephew, slumming it at the plant during the summers, getting the clean jobs. Fussed-over pretty boys who were always skipped to the front of the line, given the larger piece of the pie.

And that Volvo! How Lew hates foreign cars with their fool symbols and cheap interiors. A real car is a Caddy—a car with leg room, back support; a car that floats on air, drives like silk.

Lew's mouth feels dry and bitter from the unsweetened coffee. He looks at the clock. They've been yammering for twenty minutes. Time's up. Lew walks over and pushes open the kitchen door just wide enough to catch Kay's eyes. "I need to talk to you," he calls out.

Kay smiles at lover boy, "Will you excuse me a minute," and she gets up from the table and walks toward Lew.

Lew opens the door wider as his wife enters the kitchen.

After the door swings shut, she turns to Lew, "What is it?" Lew grabs her arm and pulls her close. "Listen," he says in a low raspy voice, "I found a dead baby—"

"What?"

Lew jerks his chin toward the living room. "In that guy's car," he murmurs, "wrapped up in a towel on the back seat." Kay cranes her neck back to look at him straight on. "What are you saying?"

"I was just checking out how they mounted the air bags and there it was."

"There what was?"

"The baby, well not exactly the baby, but an arm. I saw an arm."

"An arm!" Katya coughs out with her hand over her mouth.

"So I opened the door. I figured it had to be a doll or something."

Kay seems to waver. Lew leans into her, steadying her with his arm. "Anyway, I pulled the corner of the towel around to check it, and…there it was." Lew draws her nearer and places his lips to her ear. "You've got to get rid of him. Act like nothing's happened. Then we'll decide what to do."

Kay looks at her husband. "But—"

"That's my girl." Lew squeezes her tight then loosens his grip. "I need to write down the license. As soon as I take down the number, I'll go into the dining room. That's when you'll know to get him to leave. Understand?"

Kay stands motionless and Lew wonders if he needs to shake her. "Kay, are you listening?"

She nods and straightens her spine. "Yes," she exhales quietly.

Lew opens the kitchen door and Kay passes through.

※ ※ ※

Austin is leaning back in his chair, looking closely at his palms. "I think I found something," he says.

A shiver passes through Katya. Lew has found something too.

"See," the young man says, and points to a spot.

Katya hunches over him. It's a star, tiny but perfectly formed with a center and six off-shooting lines, and it's in the oddest place—on the Plain of Mars, right in the middle of the hand.

"That's interesting," she says not wanting to upset him. "Stars are fortuitous, a very good sign. Money, fame, fortune. Yes, and lucky too. The whole nine yards, I'd say."

Was she talking too fast? Was she making any sense? How many times has she watched police shows where the murderer or rapist or devil-worshiper was like the guy next door. Just like her guy here.

The young man beams.

She glances down at him, trying to find something she may have overlooked, some telltale sign. Maybe a tattoo, or pierced hole somewhere, or blood flecks on his shirt or pant cuffs or socks.

But all she sees is a neatly-pressed man. And she wonders if he is perhaps too clean—the kind of man who leads an obsessive life, who, at the slightest provocation, could fly into a rage if anything was out of place.

Katya takes a deep choppy breath.

"Aren't you going to sit back down?" he asks.

"Yes, of course," she says and she slides into her chair.

The man moves his hands across the table.

Katya doesn't want to touch them. Where have these hands been? Wrapped around the baby's neck, shaking the child senseless?

"Is anything wrong?" he asks.

Beads of sweat drip down her sides. The man stares at her, waiting. She must say something.

She blots her cheeks with the back of her hand. "I seem to be getting a hot fla—" and she stops. Lew's coughing in the dining room.

"Where's that sugar?" he finally calls out.

"Excuse me, won't you?" Katya says, and she pushes her chair from the table. As she stands up, the table rocks, and his empty tea cup tips onto its side.

She rushes to Lew and whispers, "Did you get it?"

"Yes," he says quietly, then adds in a normal tone, "I see it now."

Katya returns to the table and stands beside the young man's chair. Looking out at the lake, she says, "I'm afraid time's up."

He peers up at her, then reels around and shifts his eyes at Lew. "Oh…okay. How much do I owe you?"

Katya flusters. She doesn't want to fiddle for change or touch his money. "Whatever you think is fine."

He reaches for his wallet, fishes out a twenty-dollar bill and places it on the table.

"I'll walk you out," Lew tells him from across the room.

Austin pushes his chair away from the table and rises up. "Thank you," he says to Katya, extending his hand. She skims her hand through his, barely touching.

"This way," Lew says.

The two men leave the room.

Katya collapses into the couch. She feels strangely and remembers the oddest thing—the feeling she had as a young girl, leaving the movie theater in the afternoon, with the sun blinding her eyes and her wondering what was real and what was fake.

She glances around her living room and all its familiarity dims.

᭧   ᭧   ᭧

Lew leads Austin through the kitchen and out the back door. They walk silently to the car.

Dead Babies. Lew's heard about them regularly on the six o'clock news while he sits in front of the TV with his metal tray and nightly baked potato. News stories of babies discarded—some left in oven-hot cars, others strapped in watery back seats; the rest, plastic-wrapped and thrown in dumpsters. Babies baked, drowned, suffocated. All of them dead.

Lew looks down at the man's brown shoes. Leather tassels bounce from side to side with each step.

Rat-stinking murderers. That's what Lew thinks of baby killers. Just like this kid Austin. He could fit the profile. After all baby killers looked normal. He's seen it for himself, once the paper bags were taken off and the cameras got a clear shot. Fresh-cut hair, scrubbed faces, straight teeth, just like they've come from Sunday service.

Austin opens his car door and slides in.

Lew steps back. "Have a nice drive."

Austin leans forward. "Sure thing," he says and he rears out of the driveway in choppy fits and starts. From the perch of the main road, Austin casts a wave in Lew's direction.

"Ciao," Lew says to himself and he watches the car charge down the speckled road that's part-sun, part-shade. At the corner, the brake lights flash twice before the car veers out of sight.

Good riddance, Lew thinks, and he glimpses at his watch. He figures five minutes to wash up and ten minutes to get there—that will give him just enough time.

Of course he'll have to tell Kay he made up the dead-baby story. And maybe he did go a bit too far. But she had promised to be done in a half an hour and she was nowhere close. Besides she had made him angry. First the sugar, then the kid, not to mention all that garbage about Venus and Mars.

Lew saunters to the house. He has to come up with a good reason. Maybe he could say it was a joke. After all he was a funny guy. He steps into the kitchen.

"Is that you?" Kay calls out.

"The one and only," Lew answers as he enters the living room.

For the first time that day, Lew notices how stuffy the room seems to be. Closed-in and warm, too warm. He should open up a window and let some air in, stir it up a bit and blow all the room's loose ends, those silly pieces of cloth off into a corner. Kay's sitting on the couch, slumped over. Dark blue lines streak down her cheeks.

"What happened to your face?" he asks.

"Is he gone?"

"Like ticker tape."

Kay dabs her eyes with a corner of her shawl. "How can we be sure he won't come back?"

Lew reaches into his pocket, pulls out a square white handkerchief and sits next to his wife. "Here use this," he says, offering his hanky.

Kay takes it and blows her nose.

"Listen, Kay, about that kid—"

"Was it a little boy or a little girl?" she asks between gasps of breaths.

"Huh?"

"The baby."
"Oh."
"Was there blood?"
"No, no blood. Listen Kay—-"
"Then why was it in a towel?"
"Towel?"
"You said the poor thing was wrapped up in a towel."
"Well, that's what I said but—"
"Were there bruises?"
"No bruises, no blood, no nothing."
"Nothing?"
"Right…nothing."
There. Lew was halfway, just two more words—no baby.

She gazes at him wide-eyed, her eyes filling up again and for a moment, Lew sees her thirty years younger. Her face blushed and round. A thick tear collects in the corner of her eye and falls down her cheek. She leans into him, resting her head on his chest. A tingling sensation ripples inside him.

"Well, maybe it was an accident," she says, sniffling." Maybe the little angel died of crib death or swallowed something or was sick with a fever." His wife, all wrinkled and damp, looks into his face. "That's possible right?"

Lew circles his arm around her shoulder and presses her close. She collapses into him and runs her arms along his waist, nestling her face under his chin.

He's forgotten how she feels, so warm, so soft. And her touch brings back memories of a different time. The pavilion down at the lake, the yellow lights, the slow dance.

"Lew," she says, "do you think it could have been an accident?"

An accident, Lew thinks, yes of course. A verbal accident, that's what the lie was, nothing more, nothing less. An oral kink, a blurb. Something that simply fell off the shelf. No one's fault, no damage done.

She arches her head back and speaks into his ear. "Are you listening?"

And he is, sort of, but not to her words so much as to her rhythms—her breath, heart, pulse; eavesdropping like some thief who breaks in and hears the dripping faucet, the ticking clock, of an empty house. "Sh," he tells her.

Lew can't remember the last time he's held her.

"Yes, that must be it," she says to herself. "Of course, what other reason could there be?"

Her hair smells flowery like roses.

"He couldn't have done such a thing on purpose," she continues.

But Lew isn't paying much attention. He tilts his head and presses his lips to her forehead, then to the bridge of her nose. Suddenly she sits upright.

Lew reaches for her, wanting to tow her in, wanting to bring her back but she stands up; she slips away.

She steps over to the window and sighs. "He seemed like such a nice boy."

Nice boy? What planet was Kay on? Couldn't she see how the kid was playing up to her like some kiss-ass Casanova—opening doors, grabbing her, and all the time grinning like some goon.

Lew slaps his hands on his lap. "Kay, nice boys drive around with dirty laundry and baseball mitts in their backseats. Not dead babies!"

"Yes, of course," she says quietly not bothering to turn around. The light from the window makes her appear small and round-shouldered.

Lew rests his elbows on his knees and considers the braided rug with its winding circles. Somehow he got sidetracked, made a left turn. Is it too late to go back? He rubs his face.

When he looks back up Kay is in front of him. She kneels down and drapes her arms on his folded legs.

"You're right," she says, looking into his eyes. "And not just about him but about everything."

"Everything?"

"You know, about having strange people come to the house."

Could it be that Kay is finally coming around to his way of thinking—to forget this mystic stuff and get on with real life. "Yeah, it's like I've been telling you, but you never listen. There's just too many screwballs loose."

Kay blinks. "I should've listened to you."

He draws her in again. She doesn't resist. "Everything is going to be fine," he tells her.

He closes his eyes, strokes her back and tightens her between his legs.

She speaks into his ear. "Should I call 911 or do you want to?"

A jolt goes through him. His eyes pop open.

"And I suppose they'll be wanting the license number."

The license number! He hadn't bothered writing anything down. He loosens his grip and leans back. "Now Kay, settle down a minute. Maybe phoning wouldn't be such a good idea. Everyone in town with a scanner will pick up the dispatch when they send a car over. He's still out there, you know. No telling what he might do if he finds out we're the ones who blew him in." Lew shakes his head. "This can't be handled over the phone."

"I suppose so," Kay says as she rises to her feet. "I'll wash my face then we'll leave."

Lew jumps up. "No definitely not," he blurts out. "I'll go down there myself. You shouldn't be involved. You've done enough already. Besides what more could you tell them?"

"Well, I could tell them about his hands."

"His hands?"

"His lines, you know, and my impressions."

Lew feels an argument coming on. "I don't think they'd be interested."

"You mean they'd think I was crazy."

"I didn't say that."

"But that's what you meant," she says tearfully.

"I just think we should stick with…the facts. There's no reason for you to get involved. I'll handle it."

Kay drops onto the couch. "I do seem to have a headache."

"All the more reason for you to stay home."

"But what if he comes back?"

Lew feels the room closing in on him. Suddenly, the air is too thick to breathe.

"No way, that kid's gone for good," Lew reassures her. "He took off like a bullet when I told him I was a retired FBI agent."

"You what?"

"Well, I had to tell him something. You know, to make him think twice about messing with us."

Kay shakes her head. "But an FBI agent—really, Lew."

"It worked. The minute I told him, he got in his car and took off. In fact, he was so nervous, he almost flooded the damn thing."

Kay gazes at her husband. "When do you think you'll get back?"

Lew eyes his watch and figures in the time. "Shouldn't take me more than an hour."

"And what about the Noonans?"

"The Noonans…of course, well, I'll have to call them and cancel."

His wife shivers in the corner of the couch and tightens the shawl around her.

"You'll be all right?" he asks sheepishly.

Her face sags, and for a brief moment Lew imagines staying home. "I'll get you a blanket," he says, sidestepping into the dining room. "Put your feet up." He opens the bottom drawer, pulls out a blanket and goes back to cover his wife.

"I'll call you from the station," he says, tucking her in. "I won't be long." He then stretches over, plucks the telephone from a small table and places it on the floor beside her.

Kay lays the back of her hand along her forehead, nods silently, then closes her eyes.

Lew turns to leave. "I'll lock up," he says.

❦   ❦   ❦

Driving north on Route 60, past the vineyards and the trailer parks, Lew wonders what went wrong. His intention to tell Kay the truth was there but somehow it got waylaid. It must have been her tears. What was it about a woman crying that made you want to say anything, do anything? He couldn't kick her while she was down. He did the right thing, the only thing under the circumstances. Besides, maybe she learned a lesson, got a wake-up call.

Anyway, he'd make it up to her somehow.

Lew rolls down the car window. Fresh spring air swirls around him, blowing his hair onto his forehead. He makes a mental note to comb his hair in the motel parking lot. Then he twists off his wedding ring and drops it into his left breast pocket.

❦   ❦   ❦

Author's note:

This story is the premise of an unfinished novel. A lie is told that quickly sets the plot on a rocky road. Both Katya and Lew remind me of two good people who are not necessarily good to each other. (Hmmm, that resonates.) Anyway, perhaps what makes life tolerable is the comfort of habits. But in a long-term marriage, such habits can breed indifference, a blindness to the eventful possibilities that happen each day.

Nobody who has read this story likes Lew. Of course that's good because by the end of the novel, he's the one who changes the most and becomes the hero. Still, even in this shorter rendition, I empathize with him. Okay, he's a surly, womanizing schmuck, but his head's on straight. And, as it turns out, Austin's way shadier.

"The Accident" was first published in The Southern Cross Review.

Luck

Some people were simply charmed with an overabundance of luck, serendipity. Who could explain it? Georgina Mars was one such person. Whether it was finding a ten dollar bill along a curb, or getting her name picked out of a raffle box, she often found herself in the right place, at the right time for no particular reason.

It was a late Wednesday afternoon and on her way home from the hospital where she worked, Georgina stopped by the local library to look for hor d'oeuvre recipes for her niece's baby shower. There she found a dog-eared Betty Crocker cookbook. Opening to appetizers, she scanned the selections: deviled eggs, Jello molds, ham salad. Her face scrunched up as she wondered, did people still eat ham salad sandwiches? Suddenly, a man planted himself next to her, uncomfortably close.

Georgina readjusted herself in her seat. Fleetingly, she cast a glance around. There were several empty chairs and her first thought was that he could be a very lonely man. But what could he possibly do in a public place? Not much, she consoled herself, and returned her attention to celery and all its stuffings, peanut butter, cream cheese, tuna.

Without warning, the man leaned into her. "I need your help," he whispered.

"Excuse me?" she asked.

His eyes darted left and right, then something was slipped onto her lap from beneath the table. A moment later, he bolted from his seat and rushed through the double doors into the street.

Georgina felt the weight of the package and froze. What was happening here? She took a shaky breath, pushed her chair away from the table, and looked down fearfully. Whatever it was, was wrapped in plain brown paper. Her mind raced. Could it be a bomb? Was she about to be blown to smithereens in the most unlikely of places? She considered calling out or screaming fire but no, she was in a library and couldn't bring herself to speak louder than a whisper.

Gingerly, she raised the package off her lap and placed it onto to the table. There, she thought as her heart pounded. Now all she had to do was stand up and walk away. Let someone else deal with whatever it was. But something stopped her. A frail script written in jittery blue ink letters read, *Georgina*. A chill ran through her. She looked in the direction of the front door, hoping to see the man again. Was he someone she had known? An old boyfriend, grayed and wrinkled beyond recognition? Was the package a gift, long forgotten? It was unlikely, but what other explanation could there be? Well, there was one way to find out. She closed the cookbook, placed the package under her arm, and went home.

At the kitchen table Georgina slipped her fingers beneath the folds of the package and loosened the wrapping, exposing a shoe box. Carefully she lifted up the lid and found it filled with packing popcorn. What if there was something alive inside? A snake, a black widow spider? She eyed the contents closer, debating whether to pluck out each curly-cue piece or dump the lot of it. She opted for the latter and, grasping the box carefully, she went over to the kitchen sink. With an extended arm, she flipped the contents into the basin. The popcorn spread out, exposing a brick, red and weathered. How odd indeed.

Taking a set of tongs, she dug around its perimeter then flipped it over. It was an ordinary masonry brick. Nothing was taped to it, or written on it, or hidden by it. Georgina stood back and wondered, was it a sign? Coal inside a Christmas stocking came to mind. That night she couldn't sleep and at 2 AM, she took the brick to her rear window and threw it away.

❦   ❦   ❦

Roger McCulver felt lucky on certain days and on those days, he'd take some extra chances; chances like being outside when it was still daylight. Roger fished usually by night, but sometimes he went out earlier to see how the biting was. Before he left home, he chose his bait and readied his line and hook. In this case a brick inside a box.

Roger fished for women, not to eat of course, how crude; but to murder—for sport. Oh, he wasn't proud of his peculiar pastime, but it was more fun than whittling or squeezing the pus from his boils.

In his twisted mind, his victim chose herself. How? By wearing her name. It could be stamped on a license plate, embroidered on a bag, or printed on a name tag. He then snagged a woman's interest by giving her a parcel, nicely personalized.

On this particular day, Roger went to the library. Two candidates cropped up in less than five minutes: *Suzie* the librarian, who sat behind the counter, and *Georgina* the nurse, who worked at St. Mary's. While in the men's room, he made his choice, *Georgina*, and scribbled her name on the package. After dropping it onto her lap, he left the library, waited outside, then followed her home.

Georgina lived a short two blocks away in a three-story apartment building. For several hours, he watched her through his binoculars. And once the moon was high and bright, he made his move toward the fire escape that lead to her apartment.

His beating heart thudded as he began his ascent. In the distance a window slammed shut and suddenly, for reasons only kismet can explain, a heavy brick pommeled his head, knocking him over the guard rail and to his precipitous and poetic death.

Author's note:

Invisible black ice hardens on the road. A young mother, with kids in the backseat, tailspins and the family car smashes into a tree. Officers lament, "wrong time, wrong place". I like to think we miss the bullet more times than not and, in the end, evil will succumb to innocence.

"Luck" is the only story I wrote without knowing the ending first. After Georgina threw the brick out the window, I laughed at my folly, hit the Save button, and figured "Luck" would find a home in the recycling bin. But, after a night's sleep, I awoke with the idea of a different POV. Suddenly, Roger was born, then died in record time.

"Luck" was first published in Nefarious-Tales of Mystery.

The License Plate

The day had begun with Barbra, the cat, jumping on the dresser in her normal disruption; a swat here, a swat there, first nudging, then bunting, tubes of lipsticks over the edge and onto the floor with a clatter. Jessie opened her eyes, rolled onto her back and stretched before turning to look at her husband, shirtless and diagonal on the bed, like the way he cut his sandwiches.

He was a handsome man, a sleeping prince. How else could she describe him with his solid, symmetrical good looks? What was it about men in general, and David specifically? The muscle mass, she assumed, and its taut closeness to the skin. She watched his diaphragm rise and fall. It was as if his body had been chiseled from the smoothest marble and lovingly rubbed and buffed by a fine renaissance artist into timeless perfection. His wide shoulders curved gently, but with certainty, into biceps that even at rest, swelled. So unlike her own body which was altogether too fluid and malleable by hormones, water retention, and, as she now understood, the tentativeness of her own convictions.

Jessie's marriage bellied-up that morning, quite unexpectedly. Well, bellied-up may be an exaggeration since it didn't really turn over like some white-stomached whale that is rolled back into the sea after it jumps shore and dies for no apparent reason. *Quick-sanded* would be a better expression since the end of her marriage was quiet and irrevocable; a gravitational pull downwards, where a thick blanket of unbreatheable space engulfed her, and her marriage, into some vague but certain vortex until she, and it, were no more.

It happened on a Sunday, their assigned day to relax and read the newspaper to one another. Movie reviews, stock quotes, and aloud ponderings of seven-letter words for inclement weather—drizzle, thunder. Interspersed among these, was their ongoing discussion of what color to paint the hallway. After six months they still couldn't decide. What impression did they want to project? Hallways, David had reiterated (and Jessie had agreed), were signature rooms, statements of character, like the front door, which had taken a year and a half to settle on—black raspberry, not quite red, not quite purple, deepened with a hint of dark blue undertone.

Jessie tried to recollect what he had first said that morning. Something mundane she was certain, some comments about the weather most likely. Was it raining? Was it supposed to rain? Did it rain last night? At which time point she had probably turned the kitchen curtain aside and looked out. But the sun was shining. It was so bright, her eyes ached. That much she remembered, positively, for sure.

Jessie thought of leaning over and running her mouth across his chest, tasting his salt with her tongue. But David, unlike any other man she had ever known, didn't like anything that remotely suggested sex before either of them hadn't properly showered and brushed their teeth. The quick roll would have to be postponed until after breakfast or perhaps snuck in before the eggs were scrambled.

She denied herself and her appetite for the moment, rolled from the bed, plucked some clothes from the dresser, and headed for the spare bedroom.

They had set up the extra space as an exercise room. A Nordic track and stepper took up opposite corners. Double green mats lay in the center with three sets of hand weights at their side. Jessie closed the door tight to lessen the sound of the creaky hardwood floor. She then stripped off her nightshirt, straightened the towel she had left several days earlier, and positioned herself for twenty minutes of reps.

Lying naked on the floor, she ran her hand across her stomach. How flat and tidy her insides became with the help of gravity. She looked from the lower edges of her eyes and saw, between the slight mounds and undefined peaks of her breasts, an unencumbered view to her toes. She bent her knees, crossed her arms and began with crunches.

At first it was easy, good form, even breaths, but after one-hundred and fifty, the burn settled in and slowly her form dissolved. She pushed forward for another twenty-five. Each curl slowly disintegrated, too high, too low. Her shallow breaths raced. Ten more, she tried, but quit at six. She stretched out and felt her heart pounding. Sweat dripped from her underarms. She rolled over, propped herself on her side, and began scissor-leg lifts.

Exercising had been an unnatural state for Jessie. Unnatural, boring, and time-consuming, that was, until she met David, who was an avid runner. Three years later, she now cross-trained with sixty mile bike rides, two mile jogs and, whenever she had a few extra moments, a hodgepodge of aerobic and muscle defining exercises. What she looked forward to the most, however, was when her workout ended, when her body gave up.

She rolled to the other side and began again. Her forehead was sopping; drips fell onto the terrycloth towel. She was going to push herself today since she had cheesecake at work on Friday. She had to keep reminding herself to align her back and not lean forward. Between each lift, she thought specifically about her body position and made minor adjustments.

Once finished, she steadied her breathing and slowly recovered. Soon, she felt invigorated and wiped the sweat that now covered her body. As her hands passed over her breasts, the tissue changed. Suddenly she had a naughty thought.

She stopped for a moment and listened quietly for David. She then imagined him coming to watch. How silly to be concerned or guilty. But she was a married woman, and it was not something she needed to resort to. Laying quietly, she breathed deeply, and thought of the ramifications. Would she tell him at breakfast? Present it as a hypothetical? "Honey, what if your wife pleasured herself while you slept?"

Jessie smiled at his possible reaction. He'd crook his head to the side, take a sip of coffee and ask, "Pleasured? Do you mean jerked off?" And a conversation would follow not about the act, but what to call the act, "jerked off" being the point of departure; whereupon the question would arise if a woman could, by nature, jerk off. Jessie thought about this for a moment—semantics could be prickly.

She decided to forego any immediate pleasure, and took a steaming ten-minute shower followed by a twenty-second cold rinse to close her pores. She rubbed herself dry, then erased the fog from the full length mirror with the damp towel. Standing back, she appraised her body.

David and she did have secrets. Did he have any idea that after she ate, her waist expanded two inches? Did he ever notice the occasional, corkscrew hair that she missed while shaving? Quirky habits lurked below the surface, awaiting their turn to reveal themselves. Jessie smiled and thought of the marriage vow…for better or worse.

Running her fingers through her shoulder-length hair, she blew the wetness dry. She bent over, shook her head, and spritzed a light volume-enhancing spray near the roots of her hair. Once upright, she perfumed her brush and raked it along the underside of her hair near the nape of her neck.

David liked her natural looks, but natural was deceptive. The blond highlights in her light brown hair needed six-week touch-up, and her doe-like blue eyes, large and almond shaped, were more the by-product of smokey eye shadow and midnight liner, than anything she could have possibly been born with.

She pulled on a pair of faded jeans and tucked in a white, oversized, button-down shirt. The soft cotton felt comforting against her skin, and the clean smell cleared her mind momentarily of the never-ending rehash of her imperfections.

She padded down the stairs in her socks, careful not to slip on the gleaming, honey-colored steps.

They had decided to forego the honeymoon (a Winnebago rental and cross-country trip), to have all the wall-to-wall carpeting removed and the hardwood floors refinished. While she had always dreamed of traveling light with someone she loved and a 35 millimeter camera, David had convinced her otherwise, saying that floors, like walls, were canvasses, the basic building blocks for designing and defining a living space that went beyond the visual; a presence that was both seductive and strong, like white, straight teeth. Jessie didn't argue the point. How could she? The beauty of the floors provided, not only tangible pleasure, but a solid foundation from which to build—the perfect metaphor of their marriage.

Jessie quietly opened the front door, collected the newspaper, and continued into the kitchen. She then poured herself a large glass of water, set the table, and settled into her Sunday morning ritual.

David didn't cook, nor did he having much interest in cooking. That was her realm. So before breakfast, and while she waited for him, she reviewed the weekly food ads, checked the sales, and planned their evening meals.

Her eyes darted up and down the pages and in no time she had a list: Caesar salad, grilled salmon, pasta with broccoli; She then added jambalaya with a question mark. (Shrimp and sausage were on sale, but she had been avoiding any dish with okra.) Underneath, she wrote Chinese take-out.

As she cut out the coupons, he stirred. Footsteps sounded overhead, a door opened, water rumbled through the pipes. She looked at the clock. He'd be getting ready for his fifteen-minute run. She got up, cut two oranges in half, and got out the plastic juicer. His hurried steps lumbered down the stairs. She turned.

He wore a Notre Dame T-shirt and a pair of gray sweats. His hair was brushed back and slightly wet. She imagined that he had thrown water on his face after he had brushed his teeth, and with his hands still wet, had run them through his hair. As she squeezed the oranges, he sidled up behind her, put his arms around her waist, and kissed the nape of her neck.

"Looks good, smells good," he said.

"The juice?"

His hand cupped her breast and a finger reached into the vee of her shirt. "Yeah, that too."

She turned to kiss him, but he stepped back.

"Gotta run. How's the weather?"

She reached out and pulled the curtain aside. The sunshine was blinding. It was a beautiful, uncomplicated day.

He smiled boyishly with a wink and a slight grin. She handed him the small glass of juice. He swallowed it in two quick gulps, and before she could ask him what he wanted in his omelet, the door slammed.

She opened the refrigerator door and wondered what she should surprise him with. An omelet of course, but should she add capers, onions? Or just stick with the spinach, portobelloes, and baby swiss. She pulled it all out along with the eggs, butter, and cream. Sundays were cholesterol days.

By the time David returned, she had the ingredients chosen and the table set.

He barreled into the kitchen from the back door, and while she set up the coffee, he did some cool-down stretches.

"Good run?"

"Great."

David had several two-mile courses measured out. "Which route did you take?"

"Sheridan."

He stretched into a lunge position and bounced on one knee. "You're not going to believe what I saw."

Jessie looked into his face. He had barely broken a sweat. His dark brown eyes wrapped around her heart.

"Down in the Denny's parking lot there was this couple getting out of their van. Florida plates, bumper stickers up the wazoo. Niagara Falls, Grand Canyon…Get the picture?"

She nodded, and saw in her mind's eye two retirees, who argued about directions and cuddled at night.

"Anyway, get this, their license plate said *Bud & Jo*." And he roared.

Jessie smiled.

He reached over and grabbed a piece of cheese. "Man, is that tacky or what!"

It was tacky, she supposed, but an endearing tacky. "Sounds cute," she said.

"Cute? Are you serious?"

She sliced the mushrooms. "Well, I don't see the harm in it. I mean—"

"Jess, why would two people advertise their relationship like that. What's the point, except to look like idiots."

Jessie shrugged her shoulders as she whisked the eggs. "Were they an older couple?"

"Old enough to know better."

Jessie put down the fork and turned to him with feigned concern. "Does that mean I should forget about monogrammed towels for Christmas?"

He leaned up against the counter, and thought for a moment. "Initials are okay, I suppose, if they're done in private."

She wanted to ask him if he were serious, but instead she reached for his arm and drew him close. "Private? Like here?" And she kissed his soft, wet lips.

He stiffened and pulled away. "Listen, got to take a shower. Then maybe we can do it."

Jessie reeled back, feeling her smile fade. "Excuse me?"

"Come on, Jess, I'm all sweaty. Can't you hold off a few minutes?"

"I can hold off a lot longer than that."

His eyebrows rose, then his face tightened. "Fine," he said and he walked from the room.

Jessie grabbed onto the counter to steady herself. What had just happened? Not a fight or an argument, but something more disturbing, a foundational shift, a hair-line crack in fine bone china.

It was her own voice saying, for once, what she truly knew. They would never rent a Winnebago, or go on a cross-country trip, or have their names imprinted on a license plate.

Barbra, as though sensing her distress, rubbed against her leg and purred softly.

❦ ❦ ❦

Author's note:

Relationships are fodder for fiction. An "innocent" remark is made between a couple, and abruptly the relationship disconnects and bobs in unchartered territory. The reaction to this story splits down gender lines. Men say "huh?", while women nod knowingly.

It's been researched by linguists that men and women communicate differently. Subtleties are lost on men, while women interpret men's comments as brusque and insensitive. How are relationships maintained through this confusion? Apparently, for Jessie and David, not well.

"The License Plate" was first published in The Southern Cross Review.

EE O NAA

Jenna Wheeler reaches under her spare pillow and pulls out the vial. Its slender bottle with tiny cork and rounded bottom sits in the palm of her hand like the smallest of magical wands. She pinches it carefully, reverently, then lifts it to the window. The dark green liquid, opaque as velvet, brightens into a deep emerald shade when held to the light. Mesmerized, she twists and turns it as the warm, thick luminescence laps, then dissolves down the glass sides.

Her long wait is about to end. She closes her eyes and rolls the small cylinder between her hands. Her lips form an exhaling breath while she meditates. Within moments the energy of the love potion expands, warming her palms. With deep concentration, she wills its heat up her arms and into her heart. "EE O NAA" she hums quietly, bathed in the mantra she lifted from the middle of his name.

For three and a half years, Jenna has been trying to get a man to fall in love with her. Well, not just any ordinary man, but specifically, Leonard Hartnett, her sometime boss in the mail room where she works. She's tried everything from the obvious to the ridiculous, and a little beyond, if that were possible, but then sleeping for three months with a shoe she had stolen from his apartment, or lying within a triangular configuration of burning incense and tree bark at four in the morning with the hope of astroprojecting herself into his heart, might just qualify.

But such misguided attempts were months ago, having been driven, she would now say, by erratic hormonal levels that have since quieted from jagged peaks and valleys to smoothed rolling hills, copasetically green. Thanks to a psychic named Verishna, Jenna now has proper counsel as well as a money-back-guarantee to finally, and categorically, make her wish come true.

Jenna makes a mental check. Not only are the planets aligned, her Venus with his Mars, but certain small but significant karmic events have foreshadowed that the time is ripe. Specifically, in the last forty-eight hours, a telemarketer referred to her as Mrs., and Marie from next door brought her two tomatoes instead of one.

Jenna exhales a cleansing breath and visualizes how it will be in less than ten hours, the true beginning of their life together. Her eyelids flutter as the fantasy materializes.

What she envisions is Leonard in loungewear from Calvin Klein, an immaculate, metallic gray robe and pajama set, that, while satiny to the touch, is both manly and blatantly suggestive. The robe is untied, the pajama top, unbuttoned. Does he have hair on his chest? Yes, she decides, the softest brown fleece, not too much, not too little, that climbs up from his washboard stomach and spreads symmetrically across his chest. She sighs deeply and wonders if she should take her visualization further, further in a downward direction. But the drawstrings on his pajama bottoms will have to be toyed with at another time. There are still some preparations that need attending before she must leave for work and set her plan in motion.

She reopens her eyes and looks around her bedroom. Tapered, cream-colored candles, the kind that drips molten wax down the sides like heavy brocade, stand clustered in golden brass holders. She lit them the previous night before undressing in the vanity mirror to see the full effect. She wasn't displeased. Their flickering glow made her dull, brown eyes glisten, and her normally hard, angular edges softened and gently curved in the smokey shadows.

But now in the stark light of day, she worries how she may appear in the morning when she awakens in his arms and gazes into his eyes.

After all, according to Verishna, this is when the everlasting love spell will be finalized, when the love potion will take its final effect.

She rises from the bed, angles her mini-blinds closed, and yanks the curtains shut. The room is shrouded in quiet, fading color. Perfect. Her only remaining concern is what to wear to a not-so-ordinary day at the office.

Two new sets of bras and panties lie on the bed, one black, one red. It was an easy decision to forego any tan or pink undergarments which, in the store's flourescent lights, made her skin appear an anemic shade of dishwater gray.

Dropping the robe from her shoulders, she stands with her back to the mirror and changes into the red ensemble for the third time this morning. She slips on the panties, fastens the bra, then turns to face her image.

Red is not usually her color, too harsh, too look-at-me, but in a room with little light, the cherry red radiates a shimmering glow that is, for lack of a better word, succulent.

It's seven-thirty, and she only has a few minutes to make a final decision. Standing back, it comes to her: black for smoke, red for fire. And red it stays.

🍁   🍁   🍁

At eleven o'clock, Leonard breezes into the mailroom.

When Jenna first met him, she thought he was vaguely odd looking, his face, a bit too round, his eyebrows, overly dark and thick. But as time passed, these features made him cuddly, like a bear cub, and the sexiest man alive.

Today, his jacket is off and his shirt sleeves are rolled up. The sight of his hairy forearms makes her ache.

Jenna turns her eyes toward her work—triple fold, insert, swipe, stack, and listens acutely for his approaching steps. Tangled up in the din of the mail machine's chug-a-lugging, her heartbeat accelerates to warp speed.

"Hey, Jenna, what's up?"

She purposely stalls for a moment, not wanting to appear overly eager, then slowly raises her head. "Oh. Hi, Leonard."

"We still on for tonight?"

"Yes, I went to Home Depot and got the fixture I liked. But it may need some assembly."

"No problem. I'll get you up and running in no time."

"Great. So I'll look for you at five?"

"Meet you here. Sure you can drive me to my car after I finish?"

"Leonard, it's the least I can do."

"See you later then," he says with a grin. He puts his hands in his pockets and saunters from the room. His stride is effortless, his bulging gluts swagger. Jenna blinks herself back to reality.

It was Verishna who had helped Jenna decide on the proper ploy to get Leonard over to the house. It was so obvious, Jenna was surprised she hadn't thought of it herself.

Leonard fixed things. Whether it was putting the tiniest screws into eyeglass frames or disassembling the copier machine to find that last ripped sliver of misfed paper, Leonard was The Man. It therefore followed that having him over to her newly purchased, fifty-year-old ranch home for some odd job seemed the best and least obvious approach.

For two weeks, Jenna spent every evening prowling the intimidating aisles at the Home Depot trying to find the perfect repair project that would keep Leonard engaged while he ingested the potion.

Having purchased a well-worn house, her list of repairs ranged from the minor to the monumental. But she had to be discriminating, nothing outside, in the basement, attic, and certainly nothing too dangerous. A place where she could play soft music and maintain a mood that was, as Verishna advised, "receptive to cosmic ions".

Something in the electrical department caught her eye. It was a brass chandelier that came packed in a very small box. She asked a salesclerk how something so large could fit into such a tiny space.

The explanation was simple. It needed assembly. He then opened the box and showed her lettered plastic packets of various sizes with seemingly innumerable bits of metal. Assembly, oh yeah, she greedily thought, hours of it.

At ten minutes after five, Jenna and Leonard are in Jenna's car heading north on Main Street.

The soundtrack from *Titanic* plays on the tape deck as they sit scrunched together in her Geo hatchback facing forward. Jenna fiddles with the volume. She wants it loud enough for some of DiCaprio's magic to seep into Leonard's subconscious, but not so intrusive as to prevent conversation.

"Thank God it's Friday," she says. "So, how was your week?"

He readjusts himself in the seat and begins to talk, first about the football pool and how Jamie down in accounting has won three times this season, and how he, Leonard, has been playing for at least five years and has never won once. Some type of record, he figures, and really bad luck.

She listens to the smooth cadence of his voice and nods with each sentence. Threaded among his words, her thoughts drift and she reviews her checklist for the umpteenth time. Remember, not more than three doses of three drops in three hours. She glances at Leonard and feels anchored.

Twenty minutes later they're in Jenna's dining room.

Leonard peers at the hole in her ceiling. "You got Romex. Not bad."

Jenna squints into the mass of wires. "That's a relief."

He takes off his jacket and hangs it on the back rung of a dining room chair. Clapping his hands together, he says, "All righty now." He then curls his fingers around a loose corner and pries open the cardboard box.

"Can I get you something to drink?"

"No, I'm fine thanks."

Jenna's smile freezes. This part isn't supposed to happen. If he doesn't drink anything, how is she supposed to give him the potion?

He reaches into the box and takes out a folded pamphlet that has *Instructions* written across in several languages. He fans through a few pages. "Doesn't look so bad."

"Good. I was worried that it would be too complicated."

"All you need for any job is common sense and the right tools."

"Oh, Leonard you're so smart." Jenna says as her stomach wrenches.

He pulls out a chair, sits down, and with the directions splayed in front of him, he rips open the bags and begins to separate the nuts from the bolts.

Jenna excuses herself to the kitchen.

Common sense rattles in her mind as she stands at the kitchen counter. Suddenly, an idea surfaces. She stretches into the cupboard for the salted nuts and potato chips. Surely, after a few handfuls of these, he'd want a drink. She sets up a tray with two bowls and a tall frosted glass of Pepsi.

Only one final step remains. She rolls out the silverware drawer. A white folded napkin lies diagonally across the stacked forks and spoons. Lifting it from the drawer carefully, she places it on the counter and pinches the fold open. Two long cylinders, the love potion and eye dropper, are nestled together. She breathes deeply. There's no turning back now.

She twists the tiny cork free then, bringing the vial to eye level, she plunges the dropper deep into the potion and pumps the tiny black bulb. Green liquid climbs up the slender tube. She lifts the dropper out and centers it over the fizzing soda. She watches, hypnotized, as each drop, one…two…three…plunks invisibly into the dark brown effervescence. She places her hands together, as if in prayer, and whispers "EE O NAA". A smile tugs at the corner of her lips. Soon she'll be able to trade that middle of Leonard for the real thing. With calculated calmness she grabs the sides of the tray and leaves.

Back in the dining room, Leonard is making disturbing progress. Already, the loopy stems of the chandelier are formed.

"My, you're really good at this."

"It's nothing."

"How can you say that? I go in the kitchen for a few minutes and look at what you've done!"

She hopes the anxiousness in her voice isn't showing. At this rate she may have to accelerate the doses.

He beams.

"Listen, you've got to have something to eat. Take a break."

"Cashews. Love those things. Well, maybe I will after all."

She sets the tray on the table and hands him the glass. He takes it easily and gulps some soda.

According to Verishna, the first manifestations of the love potion are memory loss and awkwardness. After this, laughter, difficult to control, will follow, as well as a general sense of well-being. Finally, she should expect a deep trance-like state where time loses its continuum and a Tantric communion between souls will take place.

Jenna turns on some carefully preselected music—new age melodies that weave soprano voices with deep bass drums—then takes a seat.

She nibbles on a potato chip and observes him carefully.

Leonard is absorbed with his project, but every so often between tightening and snipping, he reaches for a handful of nuts and washes them down with soda.

Suddenly, something draws her attention. His lips twist to one side, and he appears to bite the inside of his mouth.

"Is anything wrong?" she asks.

He cocks his head. "This A screw is longer than it should be."

Jenna squints across the table.

Between his thumb and index finger is a small stout metal shard that he holds up for her inspection. "See?"

She agrees.

"Now, the two B screws—" He stops abruptly, laughs, then adds, "I'm sorry."

Jenna feels a blush surface and smiles. "Don't be."

"Don't be what?"

"Don't be sorry."

He grins widely. "Why would I be sorry?"

Giggling, Jenna twists a strand of hair behind her ear.

He leans back in the chair and rocks with the rhythm of the music. "Nice stuff."

"The music?"

"Yes."

He's staring at her now, taking her in, consuming her with his gaze. Blindly, he reaches for his empty glass.

"Let me get you more."

He nods. "Sure thing."

Back in the kitchen, her hands are shaking. She refills his glass, then pours some for herself.

A corner has been turned, there is no question in Jenna's mind. His dark eyes have never settled on her so nakedly. She feels a mass of red-hot nerve endings. Adding three drops to his drink, she wonders: if she loved him before, how would she feel with a small dose of her own? With a quick pinch, a heavy bead ka-plunks into her drink. Taking a sip, she lets the liquid stay on her tongue and wash between her teeth. She then swallows. The soda glides down her throat like warm cider.

Leonard is no longer in the dining room, but stands in the corner of the living room looking at her CDs.

"Nice selections," he comments.

She hands him his glass. "Thanks."

"Mind if I play something?"

"Of course not."

He guzzles the drink then exchanges the discs and pumps up the volume. A familiar tune from high school fills the room. She feels seventeen again.

He turns to her. "Let's dance."

"Oh, Leonard. I'm not very good."

His hands reach out. "Come on. There's not much to it."

Jenna quickly drinks what's left of her Pepsi and places the glass next to his.

His arms slip around her waist, then, rather roughly, he pulls her in. Their hips come together as he guides her across the rug.

He nibbles on her ear. His warm breath gives her goose bumps. "Oh, Leonard," she moans.

He holds tight and sweeps her through the lyrics: *Do it to me one more time, once is never enough with a girl like you…*

After the song ends, he takes her to the couch and sits her on his lap. Hungrily, he kisses her mouth, then sucks her lips. His hands travel up her sweater and an electrifying jolt passes from her nipples to between her legs.

※ ※ ※

The next thing Jenna remembers is waking up naked with Leonard by her side. Light streams into the bedroom through the crack in the blinds. Her glance rivets to the clock. 7:50 A.M.

Groggy and with a headache, she finds the energy to lean over and kiss his forehead. He doesn't stir.

Scanning the room she sees the remnants of what happened. The candles were burned to the quick and their clothes lie strewn in a path that leads into the hallway. Two empty glasses sit on her bedside table. Did they have sex? She couldn't recall.

She considers Leonard's sleeping face, so angelic, so peaceful. Lifting a finger, she outlines his profile, from his hairline, to his eyes, nose, and lastly, to the soft curves of his lips. He continues his deep sleep.

Jenna stretches in bed and sighs contentedly. Her fairytale romance has a happy ending. And that's just the beginning. She lovingly covers the blanket over his bare shoulders and slips from the bed. She needs to wash up and make herself presentable.

From the looks of things, they had been in the bathroom. Candles that she used for decoration were burned deep into their small votive holders and the soft netted bag with aromatic oils was ripped apart. Wet towels, balled up, are discarded on the floor. Damn, she thinks, why can't she remember any of this?

She looks into the mirror. Other than her tousled hair and pounding headache, she appears remarkably well-rested. Her dry skin glows with a slight pink undertone. Opening up the medicine cabinet she takes out a bottle of aspirin and continues into the kitchen.

The power light on the CD player glows red. She presses the button and hears a slight popping noise. Passing through the dining room, the chandelier remains a spidery shell of shiny brass.

Once in the kitchen, she opens the fridge and reaches for bottled water to wash down the aspirin. Abruptly, her stomach lurches. On the top rack, next to the water, milk, and condiments, lies the vial, barely visible but distinct in its clear empty state. The cork top is nowhere around. She pokes her head in further. Her eyes run across the shelves looking desperately for the spill. But there are no green drops anywhere. A sinking thought disturbs her. Did they take the entire amount? Verishna had warned her repeatedly about not exceeding the dosage. Could this be why she has such a wicked headache? And why can't she remember anything? A horrifying panic rushes through her.

She bolts into the bedroom and calls his name clearly. "Leonard."

He doesn't move, not a twitch of an eye, not a moan. Gingerly she reaches out and feels his skin. It's warm. Certainly that's a good sign.

"Leonard!" she says sternly. "Time to get up."

No response.

Sweeping off the blanket, she grabs his wrist and heaves his body up. He's dead weight. She lets go and he flops back into the bed. *My God, is he unconscious?*

Her hand shakes as she hurriedly pokes 911. The silence between each ring is interminable.

❦ ❦ ❦

Three hours later, Jenna sits in a molded plastic chair in the emergency room waiting area. She has been placed there by a guard who remains seated at the door. After the ambulance brought Leonard in, she had become hysterical. "Unresponsive", "Stat", followed by a flurry of activity over Leonard's sheeted body, drove her mad.

Now, totally dried out from hours of crying, she feels calmer, and ready to take the blame. What had she been thinking?

How could she have been so stupid, gullible? Verishna lived in a trailer camp, for Christmas sake. Any fool would have realized that a true love potion would have netted the psychic a penthouse apartment in the Trump Towers. Now, the man Jenna loved, lived for, would be a vegetable, or something worse—dead.

A man in hospital greens pushes through the swinging door. "Ms. Wheeler?"

"Yes?" she mutters.

"We have good news. Mr. Hartnett is conscious now. Other than having a very bad headache, his vitals are fine."

"Thank God." Relief she has never known sweeps through her. "When can I see him?"

Leonard is in a small room by himself. The head of the hospital bed is cranked up and he's sitting with a breakfast tray in front of him. A nurse busies herself in the corner.

"Hey, Jenna."

Her breath catches in her throat. She rushes to him and kisses his cheek.

He smiles brightly. "What's that for?"

Jenna laughs nervously. How ridiculous that neither of them can remember what happened, but there'd be more memories to make once everything returned to normal. "Just happy to see you."

His dark eyes are luminous, and he, like herself earlier in the day, has a rosy glow.

The nurse comes over to bed. "I'll leave you two alone."

Leonard's glance passes beyond Jenna. "Thanks, Mia. But don't go far."

Jenna turns and glares at the woman. She is young, with poreless skin and deep almond eyes. Her long eyelashes flutter as a blush, crimson red, spreads across her cheeks.

Jenna pivots abruptly and studies Leonard. His eyes remain tangled up in the nurse's gaze.

"Was Mia here when you woke up?"

"Yes, how did you know?"

Jenna doesn't answer. Verishna's words echo in her ears. "It is only after a deep sleep, and after the eyes meet, that the final connection, the everlasting communion, is made."

Jenna steps back, stung by the two radiant faces.

"EE O NAA," she wails and collapses to the floor.

❦   ❦   ❦

Author's note:

Obsession, a mutation of love, is not pretty. I suppose when you don't have the real thing, a close facsimile will do.

Question: Is it better to be the adorer or the adoree, to do the loving or be loved. Unilateral relationships of both kinds have their down sides. And even though it ended badly for Jenna, at least she had many fantasy-filled hours of delight.

As you may have guessed, "roofies", the date rape drug, inspired some of the potion's characteristics. Still, it's not out of the realm of possibili-

ties to create a pharmaceutical love elixir. Stimulate the correct spot in the brain and even Bin Laden would be sweet on Madonna. Scary.

"EE O NAA" *was first published in Ascent Magazine, Aspirations for Artists.*

Casper's Quarry

Casper, sixty-seven years old, with cement-happy creditors down his throat, had to boost his cash flow fast. Uncle Sam's dole wasn't making a dent in his Friday-night losing streak. So while on the john he read the want ads and thought of what he liked (drinking coffee) and what he was good at (reading the paper). Nothing snagged his attention until his eyes settled on *Surveyors Wanted* and a eureka moment erupted, quite separate from the intestinal kind.

Within twenty-four hours, he had business cards made up. CASPER, YOUR FRIENDLY GHOST, CONFIDENTIAL SURVEILLANCE, CHEAP. Followed by a beeper number. He then went to AMVETS, got a Sam Spade coat, fedora hat and proceeded to do the one thing he did best–chillin'.

Two days later at a McDonalds, he sat across from a Mrs. Smith, a middle aged woman with more curves than the Khyber Pass and fingernails that could shred cheese. He couldn't say if she was or wasn't attractive since some of her parts were top notch, like her heaving jugs, but there was something about her face that suggested an imbalance, the uneven eyebrows possibly, or the floating eye that seem to look at him or maybe not.

After a quick, cross-eyed glance around, she leaned toward Casper. "It's my husband. I need to know where he goes after work."

"No problemo," said Casper, certain those were Bogie-words uttered to a breathless Bacall.

She slid a plain white envelope across the table. "Here's the retainer you asked for."

He cracked open the envelope, fingered the two fifties, and offered to buy lunch, a magnanimous gesture.

Back at the table with a couple of cheeseburgers, he took out a small flip pad, wetted the tip of a pencil with his tongue (it seemed the right thing to do) and asked questions. Twenty minutes later, he had numbers up the wazoo, all having to do with Mr. Smith: his date of birth, license plate, social security, phone and cell numbers, addresses of home, work, e-mail, and for good measure his shirt size, 20 long. Mr. Smith was a big man. This was confirmed after his wife pulled a photograph from her purse. "I took this last month. He hasn't changed."

Behind a desk a hulking guy with a stringy comb-over grimaced. Tucking the picture into his pocket, Casper's confidence grew. Titanic men had to be easier to nail, no where to hide, unable to run. Piece of cake. A rendevous was then arranged for the following day near the gazebo at River Park. There he and Mrs. Smith would exchange information for cash. Sweet.

Four hours later, Casper parked his pick-up across the street from Germ-O-Zap, a company that sold, delivered, and installed cleaning products to businesses. Mrs. Smith had told Casper that whenever the soap dispenser in a gas station restroom was pressed, a dime went into Germie's coffers. Too bad he didn't have any of that action.

At five twenty-eight, Mr. Smith, six-foot four and a conservative three hundred, exited his place of employ, lumbered into the street and came around to the driver's side of a red Le Baron. As he fiddled with his keys, a gust of wind whipped by, tossing his hair over like a flip top. Confirming a match, Casper fired up his engine.

Smitty first stopped at a supermarket. Casper thought of going in himself. Maxwell House was on sale, but he stayed put, not wanting to get stuck in a seven-item lane behind a price check, or a bad check, or some nut with expired coupons and attitude. Instead he refolded his newspaper and checked the horses. Blarney Stone, a personal favorite, had cruised in with sixty to one odds. Suddenly, Casper wondered if his run of bad luck was turning. Not only was Blarney on her game, but Casper had created a job of unlimited, untaxed cash flow that fit him better than OJ's glove.

Fifteen minutes later, Smitty exited into the parking lot with a paper bag topped off with a bunch of flowers. A couple of possibilities came to mind: maybe he had a sick mother, or maybe Mrs. Smitty wasn't the only one with a roving eye.

Smitty made a left onto Route 60 and headed north in the opposite direction of his residence. For the next forty-five minutes he didn't go over the speed limit and stayed in the right-hand lane, often getting stuck behind buses and stalled rush hour traffic. As the sun set Casper trailed the Le Baron beyond the city limits and into the suburbs where Smitty turned into a development called the Willows. There they wove down winding roads sidelined by sprawling homes and lawns the size of nine-holes, all prime assets for divorce sharkies. Smitty signaled right and eased into the double drive at 46 Hollyhock. Casper rolled passed, did a three-point and parked kiddy corner. By this time, Smitty was out of his car juggling his weight and groceries. At the front door, he made sure his hair was still there, squared his shoulders, then pressed the doorbell. The front porch light came on and the door opened. A blond bombshell appeared in black lace with enough cleavage to serve a turkey dinner. A moment later, Smitty cruised in and the door slammed shut.

Even though Casper wasn't being paid fifty bucks an hour to jump to conclusions, it seemed pretty clear that Smitty, besides being hooter-crazed, had an extra woman on his hands. And while this didn't pose a specific moral dilemma, Casper felt uneasy about getting paid by someone who was getting the short end of the stick, a case of adding insult to injury. Throughout the evening, and as he occasionally relieved himself in empty coffee cups, Casper considered his options. He could tell the truth, thereby giving the Mrs.

enough ammo for a bigger slice of alimony, or he could hedge, offering some variation of the truth like he did at poker. Bottom line was, no matter how he handled the situation, he needed the money to keep his body out of the river.

At ten-thirty, a half-dressed Smitty, carrying his sports coat and tie, slipped out the front door. He then loaded himself in his car and sped off. Casper tailed him through sparse traffic to a darkened home on the city's south side. It was a middle class neighborhood with crammed-together houses and patch front lawns. Smitty parked in the street, climbed the porch steps and let himself in. Casper wondered if the Mrs. was feigning sleep or waiting in a corner, drunk and hysterical. Over the years, the never-married Casper had seen it too many times, the wife, the girlfriend, the one getting screwed, the other being screwed. It was never pretty.

On the way home, Casper figured his take. Three hundred minus the retainer, left him with two hundred dollars for a few hours work. Suddenly, the ethical concerns of being a snitch evaporated. Bad hands were dealt, everyone had to deal.

As previously arranged, Casper drove to River Park at eleven the following morning and angled his truck into a diagonal slot that faced the river. He was fifteen minutes early so he cracked open his window, slouched down and covered his eyes with his fedora for a snooze. He had a busy day planned. Once he got the cash he was off to the races to parlay some chump change into serious dough. Friday was just around the corner and he needed to pay up before his ankles got weighted down with bricks.

No sooner had he slipped into some Zs, when the passenger door flew open by a breathless Mrs. Smith. She wore sunglasses and had a scarf wrapped around her head. A plastic shopping bag dangled from her wrist. For a moment, Casper thought of his Aunt Sophie, a Russian immigrant who ate too many piroshkis and onions.

"Hey there," she said.

"Mornin'."

She stalled, glancing at the seat that was covered with newspapers and food wrappers. "Can I sit down?"

Casper crunched everything together and stuffed the wad behind the seat. He then brushed some crumbs, old french fries, and a couple of forgotten pennies to the floor. "Sorry about the mess."

"Not a problem," she said as she clambered into the seat, huffing, puffing, and smelling like cigarettes.

After readjusting herself inside, she slammed the door hard and looked toward Casper. "So how did it go?"

Casper reached for his notepad that sat on the dash. He thought of saying, *Do you want the good news or the bad news?* but stopped since there was no good news. Instead he answered, "Pretty well, considering."

"Considering?"

"He was easy to follow. No problem there. Left work at around five-thirty, just as you said and let's see…" Casper stopped and referred to his notes. He wanted to act professional. "Went to the supermarket on Mayfield, then traveled up Route 60 to the Willows. Are you familiar with the area?"

Her fingers were nervously twisting the loopy handles of the plastic bag. She seemed to be staring ahead toward the river. "Yes, I'm afraid so."

Casper wondered if his bad news was old news. Had she hired him only to confirm her suspicions? "I suppose you know the rest," he ventured.

She covered her mouth with her hand and nodded silently.

"I'm sorry."

Sniffling, she asked, "How much do I owe you?"

Part of him wanted to say to forget it, but he needed the money more than Ozzie needed Harriet. "Two hundred."

Gathering herself together, she opened the plastic bag, removed a wallet and fished out two crisp bills.

"Listen, can I get you something?"

She gave him the money. "No, I'll be all right."

"Of course you will, but do you want a drink or something?"

"A drink? No…But there is one thing, if you wouldn't mind."

"Sure."

She pulled a creased photograph from the inside of her coat pocket. Without taking a glance, she shredded it to bits. "Could you toss this in the river for me?"

"My pleasure."

With remnants in hand, Casper exited the truck, and stepped to the guardrail. The roiling water churned with white caps. He tossed the scraps and watched as they fluttered every which way like confetti until they landed on the water and quickly disappeared. Turning back, he saw Mrs. Smith standing beside his truck. Casper looked around, wondering where she had parked.

As he approached, he asked. "Can I give you a lift?"

"No, my car's not far. I need the exercise."

"Well, all right then. It was a pleasure meeting you. If you need anything else, call me."

He reached out to shake her hand, but she didn't respond. "I certainly will." And she pivoted in the direction of the gazebo where a number of cars were parked.

Casper got back in his truck feeling as if he had just run over a stray cat. He then made a mental note to give her a call in a couple of days to see how she was managing. It was the least he could do. Meanwhile it was off to the races to pull a rabbit out of a hat, hopefully.

❦   ❦   ❦

Casper's debt was eighteen hundred smackers, owed to Lenny Pino, a former heavyweight with more grease on his body than oil in an engine. Nothing about Lenny was attractive. He stunk, picked his nose, and couldn't chew food and keep his mouth shut at the same time. But he did have one redeeming factor–he played rotten poker, that was until two weeks ago, when Lenny brought a two-inch plastic statue of the Virgin Mary, placed it on the table beside his beer, and began a winning streak nothing short of miraculous.

At first, Casper had figured it was dumb luck. The guy had rarely broken even in the previous six months. But by the second week, and after Casper had bluffed himself into a hole deeper than the way to China, something beyond random good fortune or divine intervention had to be at play, something like cheating. Unfortunately, before he could get back in the game and nail the jerk, he had to deal with Lenny's nephew and billing clerk, The Nutcracker (aka Da Nutta).

Da Nutta had called Casper the Saturday after the poker game and threatened to squeeze Casper's balls like plum tomatoes then use them as bullhead bait, a generally distasteful prospect. Casper hung up on the guy. The next day a couple of buckets of wet cement were left on his porch with a *UO-me or Else* note stuck on top. Casper wondered what good he'd be to anyone if he were blowing bubbles? A point he might be able to argue if or when his ankles were being tied.

Anyway, now on the ride to the racetrack, Casper was certain that things were going to work out better than fine. Not only did his nose itch, but Blarney Stone was running in the seventh, both great omens that a good night's sleep was right around the corner. Rather than waste money on the earlier races, Casper placed an all-or-nothing bet on Blarney and went directly to the clubhouse. There he ordered a T-bone steak and a couple of beers, a pre-celebratory blow out.

Five minutes before the race, Casper positioned himself down by the rails to savor his victory. In red and white silks, Blarney entered, number seven in the seventh gate of the seventh race. Man, she was a beauty, charcoal black with Betty-Grable legs, only longer and twice as many. As she entered the gate, her head was high and her stride was effortless. When the starting gun cracked, she bolted taking an early lead. But when she passed in front of him, Casper felt uneasy.

Even though she had fine form, her breathing was too shallow. By the first turn he could see her break stride. Suddenly, yet in slow motion, he watched her burnout, from first to fourth to seventh place till it was over–big time. Casper's stomach churned. Maybe it was the beef, maybe it was the money, but whenever Blarney tanked, Casper's luck imploded.

As soon as Casper returned home, he took two Alka Seltzers and decided that his best option was to lay low and visit his cousin Elmo for a few days. He then rummaged through the living room closet for an overnight bag. While packing a few essentials, a heavy knock stopped him cold. "Police. We're looking for Casper Tsabo."

Casper couldn't be sure if he recognized the voice, so he crossed over to the front curtains and looked out. A blue and white sat in his driveway behind his truck, and two uniforms stood on his porch.

One of the cops saw him. "Open up," he said.

Casper yelled through the closed window, "What do you want?"

"Need to speak with you about a friend of yours."

What friend? Were these guys sent by Lenny? Was Da Nutta a cop? "You got ID?" Casper asked.

Both men held out their badges. They looked legit.

Casper returned to the front door and cracked it open. One of the cops pushed through. "Sorry to bother you like this."

Casper reared back.

The guy, short, stocky with enough grease in his hair to be a card-carrying arsonist got in Casper's face. Casper rushed to judgement and nervously blurted, "Are you Nutso?"

"No, are you?" said the greaseball with a smirk.

The taller officer interjected, "We've been looking for you, Tsabo. Where you been?"

"The track."

"All afternoon?"

"Yeah. So what's this about? What friend?"

"You like to gamble Mr. Tsabo?" asked the tall one.

Casper's stomach flip-flopped. These guys had to be Lenny's goons. "Listen, officers, call me Casper. Now, about the money, have you ever considered that a dead man can't pay up?"

"Let's sit down Casper and have a little chat."

So they wanted to talk? Maybe Casper could straighten this out after all. "Yeah, sure."

The tall officer followed Casper into the living room. The greaser kept standing, looking around.

"Casper, is that your vehicle in the driveway?"

"Yep."

"Do you mind if we take a look at it?"

"Why? Oh, I get it. Collateral, right?"

The two officers exchanged glances. "Right, collateral," said the one.

Casper wasn't crazy about giving up his wheels, but truth be told, it was only worth around three hundred. "Sure, that seems reasonable."

The tall cop nodded to the short cop, who then left.

Casper settled into his lounger, feeling his muscles relax.

"This your suitcase?" said the policeman. "Were you going somewhere?"

"I was thinking of visiting my cousin."

"I see. By the way, what are those pails of cement doing outside?"

"You don't know?" Casper asked.

The officer shook his head.

"Practical joke, I suppose."

"Hmm."

The greasy cop, out of breath, entered the room. "Sam, can I see you a minute?"

Sam got up and walked out of the room. Their lowered voices rumbled from the hallway. Moments later, they returned and stood over Casper. Greaser held a card and began reading, "You have the right to remain silent…"

"What's this about? Listen, I can get the money."

The tall cop had his handcuffs out and motioned for Casper to get up. "You're under arrest for the murder of Jack Smith."

"Murder? Jack Smith?"

The cop jostled him around.

"I don't know a Jack Smith."

But as the handcuffs pinched his wrists and locked into place, Casper had an epiphany–Smitty!

Later that afternoon, Casper sat in a six-by-six foot room with two molded plastic chairs and no windows. Plenty of activity was going on in the general vicinity and whenever he heard approaching footsteps or a door opening, he'd look expectantly. Hours passed and Casper wondered if he was being iced, chilled before grilling. Not that it mattered since he had figured out the whole thing. Clearly, Mrs. Smitty had murdered her husband, any idiot could see that.

Finally, the door was opened by a suit.

"Hello, Casper. I'm Detective Mason. Call me John. How you doing today?"

Casper shrugged.

"Now before we go on, would you like to have a lawyer present?"

"Why would I need a lawyer?"

"Well, the allegations are quite serious—"

"Let's just get this over with."

"You sure?"

"Of course I'm sure."

"All right. Do you want to start or should I?"

"Go ahead."

"I'll tell you what I have, then you tell me your story. Deal?"

"Deal."

"Okay. I'll make it brief. You followed Jack Smith home, killed him with a .45, and stole his money."

"Huh?"

"Am I right or am I right?"

"How did you come up with that?"

The detective reached inside his patch pocket and pulled out a pad. "Here's the unabridged version. For several hours last night you stalked the victim until he arrived home at which time you entered his house and blew him away with a semiautomatic. You then wrapped the blood-splattered Ruger and the victim's emptied wallet inside a plastic bag and put them under the driver's seat of your truck and proceeded to the races where you gambled his money. Upon returning home, you had a bag packed for flight. As for the two buckets of cement, I suppose you realized you couldn't use them since the guy weighed a ton. Motive–serious debt owed to him and others."

Casper reeled in his chair. He had been set up by the Mrs.!

The detective continued, "So what do you have to say?"

Casper took a deep breath. "Right song, wrong singer."

"What do you mean?"

"Abridged version. It was his wife."

"Really? What's the unabridged version?"

Casper relayed everything he knew–Mrs. Smitty's suspicions, the other woman, their visit earlier in the day, his leaving the truck to throw away the picture, her opportunity to plant the gun and her husband's wallet.

After listening intently, the detective said, "There's only one problem."

"What's that?" Casper asked.

"Mr. Smith doesn't have a wife."

An unexplainable gravitational pull sank Casper's heart. He looked into the detective's eyes. "About that lawyer…"

Food at the county jail wasn't bad, especially the macaroni and cheese. His roommate, a black kid named Akeem played "fly" poker and showed Casper more tricks than a you-know-what. Late one night Casper talked about Lenny and Akeem gave Casper one simple piece of advice, "psych", which Casper planned to do if he ever got out.

Casper's state-appointed lawyer was just out of school and complained of having to pay for parking. He often was late for appointments or never showed up at all. Casper insisted he wanted a jury trial but the lawyerette wanted him to plea. His case went nowhere for weeks until Casper checked the horses. Blarney Stone was on fire again. Somewhere, somehow, Casper became convinced that he was about to be sprung.

It happened that very Sunday during rec. Akeem was shuffling the cards and Casper was reading the newspaper, when a headline caught his attention, PARTNER OF GERM-O-ZAP BECOMES COMPANY PRESIDENT. Beneath, a man's picture stared out at Casper, or sort of stared out. Casper pulled the paper closer and saw with vivid clarity–the roving eye!

Three days later, Casper got back into the poker game with two months of unspent social security checks and overdue rent. After he sat down, he pulled a four-inch statue of the Sacred Heart from his pocket, dwarfing the two-inch Virgin Mary. That night Lenny's rule was over.

❧ ❧ ❧

Author's note:

> Once in a while a character is born fully formed.
> Politically incorrect Casper, with his off-the-mark metaphors, was one such gift.
> "Casper's Quarry" was also my first short story where I had a subplot. Subplots can be tricky. I think they should be separate yet germane to the main plot. Like mixing checks with stripes, subplots provide texture.

Consider the movie "Back to the Future". The sub-plotting in this film should be the benchmark for all writers. Time travel, love interest, the school bully, family angst, all complete the whole. Not to mention, Fox's ode to Chuck Barry and "Johnnie B. Goode". A case of one genius copying another.

"Casper's Quarry" was first published in PLOTS WITH GUNS!.

Ka-ching

Whenever Randall blew into a town, he'd pick a church in an upscale neighborhood and scan its bulletin. What he looked for was a Single's function—the perfect venue for his scam.

Randall preferred woman in their forties and fifties, who were well maintained and lonely, very lonely. Yes, they were easy to spot: manicured fingers, expensive perfume, and hair coiffed and colored in the latest style. He could also zero in on the most wealthy. How? They never served cocktail sausages or stayed late folding tables and chairs.

St. Luke's Methodist was his pit stop this evening and he felt electric. The rush of the hunt and the challenge of the conquest always did this to him. With cool calculation, he surveyed the room for the best vantage point both to see and be seen. Instinctively, he maneuvered his way to the punch bowl. Here, as in the wild, watering holes were always prime hunting grounds. Dressed conservatively in a pinstriped navy suit, Randall nodded to whomever approached, but his conversation was selective. It was critical that he not get tangled up in sports talk with other men, since the ladies were then far less likely to approach him. And having a woman come to him was the best way to snag the prize of champagne wishes and caviar dreams.

As he perused the crowd, no one stood out. There was the usual array of stout church ladies in comfortable shoes and lace-collared dresses, as well as the spattering of pale young women who slumped and huddled in dark corners with worried expressions on their faces.

Then someone caught his eye—a woman in pink who entered on the arm of the Reverend and who everyone turned to look at. Yes, she might be his ticket. Everything about her said "Ka-ching" with capital dollar signs—her trim, tanned figure, short, sleek hair, and thick gold necklace that glinted in the light.

Randall casually sauntered into her field of vision. His height was always an advantage and within a minute her eyes latched onto his. Contact! Now all he had to do was wait and pretend to be prey instead of predator.

Her name, he was to find out, was Daphne and she was distantly related to the Kelloggs of Michigan. Not too shabby. Her home, left to her by her dearly departed husband, was a oceanfront property nestled behind an iron gate and sprawling stone wall. Randall learned these things and more during a coffee hour, after which time, she offered to give him a tour.

"My husband was twenty years older" she said as she opened the double doors to the master bedroom, "and even though we never had children, we had ten wonderful years together."

Sheer white curtains billowed into the room from an ocean breeze.

Curious as to the possibilities of money grubbing relatives, Randall asked, "Had either of you married before?"

Daphne adjusted some flowers on the mantle of the stone fireplace. "It was my first marriage, but his second."

"So you're a stepmother?" he ventured.

She laughed. "Heaven's no. Neither of us had children."

Relief swept through him. She was widowed with no heirs, the perfect uncomplicated history that he preferred. And it was then that Randall decided to put on the dog and woo yet another bride, his fifth.

The following day, Randall moved into a hotel suite, put a down payment on a new Mercedes, and took Daphne to dinner via a private plane to Boston. Yes, it was an extravagance but no matter what he bought, rented or charged, it would all be paid for by his future bride.

That evening her inquiries were probing. "What kind of business are you in?"

He beamed. How he loved this question! He could let his mind fabricate and weave any story he wished as long as whatever line of work he chose could conveniently take an unexpected downturn once they married. "I deal in fine art. My primary clients are German and Japanese businessmen. I have to travel a bit but it's quite lucrative."

"How fascinating," she said.

He agreed but bemoaned the fact that jet-setting across continents and spending weeks away from home was cumbersome.

Daphne sympathized, "It must get lonely."

Randall stared off and said quietly, "Yes, very."

A whirlwind romance followed and marriage plans sprouted.

Over a continental breakfast she asked, "But would you be comfortable in my husband's home?"

"Of course darling," he said.

She sighed heavily. "I just don't know if it would be right. Maybe we should have a fresh start."

Randall didn't like the sound of that but kept to himself. "Whatever you decide will be fine, dear."

She drummed her fingers on the table. "Or we could just remodel. Make the house more to your taste. Would you prefer that?"

He grinned. "Yes, that would be marvelous."

It was then decided that an indoor pool and sauna would be her wedding gift to him. And while the extensive renovations took place, she moved into his hotel suite.

One month later, their wedding day arrived. It was a crisp sunny day only clouded by one minute detail. On their way to the church, Daphne realized she had nothing blue and insisted that she gather

her mother's sapphire ring. It would only take an extra ten minutes and Randall agreed to be let off at the church and stall the Reverend.

When Randall entered the sacristy, the minister was waiting.

"I'm sorry Reverend, but Daphne had to run up to the house."

"House?"

"Yes, her place on the ocean."

"Oh, you mean the Seaview mansion."

"Of course."

"But that's not hers, she just housesits there."

Randall reeled as if blind-sided by a ten-ton rig. He then sprinted outside and saw the taillights of his brand-new Mercedes turn onto Highway 19, heading in the opposite direction to the shore.

❦   ❦   ❦

Author's note:

One of the best paying markets for short fiction is Woman's World, a magazine found at grocery store check-outs. They pay five hundred dollars for a mini-mystery(1000 words), one thousand dollars for a mini-romance(1500 words). Only one catch, the magazine receives three thousand submissions per month for eight slots. That puts the odds of getting a WW byline at .002 percent.

Ka-ching was a near hit. They hung onto it longer than a couple of weeks, then returned it with a short personal note from the editor: "Perfect, but too similar to a recent story". I was thrilled.

As a writer with a folder full of rejections, I've learned to distinguish rejections by the following hierarchy:

Preprinted: bottom of the barrel.

Preprinted with "send us more": step one.

Preprinted with "send us more" and a signature: moving up the food chain.

Preprinted with a handwritten sentence and signature: Celebrate! Remember: You can score without making a touchdown.

"Ka-ching" was first published in Over Coffee.

Birth From a Star

Red Magill's life started out in the minus column. In the back alley of the Cerulus bar, a haunt located one mile north of the Mohawk Indian Reservation, he was conceived with no words, no kisses, just a wham, bam kind of thing against a brick wall beside a dumpster. To make matters worse, within a week of his birth and after several days of post-partem drinking, his mother, Mary Margaret, fell asleep on a country road and was run over by a milk truck, leaving the helpless baby orphaned at a mournfully tender age.

Matters did not improve. Red was reluctantly taken in by his Irish maternal grandparents, neither of whom felt particularly keen on having a grandchild so clearly different from themselves. His name was spawned more from his grandfather's mean-spirited nature, than from the color of Red's hair or cheeks, which was anything but. Red grew up in a household with little conversation, less affection, comforted only by the constant blare of the television.

Unfortunately and for whatever reason, Red developed a speech impediment, a halting condition where, second, third syllables would evaporate for brief but certain moments before rematerializing garbled and swallowed up seconds later. It was beyond a stutter or a stammer; a condition so futile, so uncontrollable that by the delicate age of twelve, he simply stopped any elective speech that required polysyllabic words. His verbalizations were reduced to giving his first name, answering yes or no, and saying thanks.

As expected, due to his impoverished, unproductive speech, Red's education and job options were truncated. At sixteen, and in the same year that his grandparents moved to Florida, leaving him behind in a rented trailer, he dropped out of high school and began working odd, solitary jobs. He delivered the Penny Saver on Saturdays and, depending on the day and neighborhood, rummaged through garbage bags for bottle returns. Surprisingly and to his credit, Red was able to take care of himself from this seemingly meager existence. He lived a simple life. Besides riding his bike everywhere, he ate a lot of elbow macaroni and canned tomato soup.

Soon Red developed a clientele of sorts, those persons who would, instead of lugging bottles to the store or out to the curb, put them aside in pre-arranged spots for Red's weekly pick-up. One particular person was the Reverend Eugene Park, who did not want to broadcast the weekly amount of Labatt's Blue he actually drank.

By the time Red was twenty, he became a staple in the neighborhood, a gentle giant who waved and smiled to others as they walked their dogs or went for early morning walks. Soon he expanded his trade to cleaning gutters, washing windows, clearing out basements and attics. He did whatever he was told and only took the money that was offered.

It should be no surprise given his quiet, agreeable nature, that Red eventually got a break. It came on Thanksgiving Day from the Reverend Park, who after assuring that Red did not have a police record, offered him employ as grounds keeper and general maintenance worker at St. Matthew's Episcopal Church, a closely supervised position which entailed any and all jobs that had to be done outside, in the basement or on a ladder.

Red quickly found out that December was his busy month. In addition to his normal duties, he assisted with the church decorations. There were the obvious things: unpacking the crèche from the basement and hauling it upstairs, putting up the tree, running lights, arranging the poinsettias. He was also asked to stay late on Mondays,

Wednesdays, as well as all day on Saturday while the choir practiced. It was up to Red to make sure everything was turned off and locked up once they left. His favorite part of the job was when, after a long day, he'd sit in a back pew while the choir sang yet another chorus of "The First Noël" or "Ding, Dong! Merrily On High".

And on those same nights when the choir rehearsed, the Reverend Park, tucked neatly under his electric blanket, would listen until he was lulled exquisitely to sleep by the breathtaking harmonies: "Gloria, Hosanna in Excelsis…", "And what was in those ships all three on Christmas Day?…"

The choir at St. Matthew's was the jewel of the church. It drew worshipers from the entire city and not just Episcopalians. The Reverend Park could tell the difference as he stood outside and shook hands with the throngs of people who didn't wear conservative suits and ties, or camelhair coats. For the past three years, midnight Mass had been standing room only, and on Christmas day, two extra services besides the eleven o'clock had been added. For the first time this year, the choir had sung with the Philharmonic and now there was talk of a record deal. A windfall for the church.

It was rumored that a member of the congregation was bringing someone in from PolyGram Records to listen to the choir just this Christmas and the Reverend Park became very concerned with presentation. He ordered new cassocks, red with white surplices, and also decided to put the choir up front, to the right of the altar. Olive Prudhomme, the choir mistress, had agreed that the voices would showcase better that way.

Another idea of the vicar's was to have a huge star placed above the singers. He drew up the plan himself and drafted a blueprint on graph paper. A star of David, he envisioned, cut from a four by four, half-inch thick piece of plywood, sprayed gold and covered with one-thousand of those miniature white lights. He gave specific directions to Red and oversaw his daily progress.

The making of the star was not an easy job. Many tiny holes, measured precisely one-quarter inch apart, needed to be drilled through the plywood to secure each light. Soon it became evident however that the layout had been miscalculated and the whole undertaking had to begin again, not once but twice. Adjustments to the width and spacing of the lights were calibrated and the their final number rose to over two thousand. It was a difficult time for the Reverend as he guided Red through every redesigned step. Red, in his usual way, showed no end to his patience and did what he was told.

The final product was much heavier than what the Reverend had imagined. Still, with wire, screws and several heavy-duty extension cords, Red managed to hang their creation from the ceiling. And on the night before Christmas Eve the star was lit. Its blazing light illuminated the sanctuary with such a crushing brilliance that even the Reverend Park could not find the words to exalt its magnificence. A masterpiece.

🍁   🍁   🍁

On Christmas Eve the church was ready. The choir dressed, the organist arrived and one hour before the service, they warmed up. Red sat in his usual spot in the back of the church, dazzled by the spectacle, when suddenly, during a rousing rendition of "God rest ye merry gentlemen," the light from the star wavered as if blown by a breeze. Red imagined it was the sheer power of the voices that made the light shimmer but before he could investigate, the star shuddered, then shook, before crashing down, plummeting onto two unsuspecting male choristers, who quickly toppled backwards, disappearing from view. Olive screamed. The choir scattered, and the vicar rushed in from the rectory.

By the time Red got to the front of the church, the two young men were sitting up on the floor, half-dazed amidst the startled group. Red stood off to the side with his head hung down. Surely St. Matthew's chance for fame and fortune was not to be this year. He uttered an apology, "Sor..." but nothing more came out.

The Reverend and Olive fired off orders. An ambulance was called and the choir quieted. Red swept up the shattered plastic bulbs, gathered what was left of the star and carted its remains into the basement, passing the Reverend Park and Olive who were in the sacristy, their heads huddled together.

Red wanted to help, but how? and quietly while in the damp, dark basement, he began to sing Avé Maria in a tone so rich and mellifluous that the floor vibrated underneath where the vicar and Ms. Prudhomme stood. The Reverend Park recalled that same voice from his dreams. He reached out and grabbed Olive's arm as they silently listened to the deep resonance that spanned two octaves. They flew down the stairs to find Red. Olive's only question was, "Can you read the words?" He nodded, and without forethought, they dressed him in a crimson robe.

Six-foot three-inch, two-hundred and fifty pound, ragged black-haired Red positioned his ungainly frame in the last row of the choir and for a moment, he felt disoriented and somewhat dizzy. Whether these sensations were caused by seeing the church from a different angle, or feeling the heat of a thousand eyes, he couldn't quite say. His breath quickened as a man close-by nudged him to open his song book to page one. His vision blurred, then focused—Silent Night.

Olive stepped to the front of the choir, her hands in mid-air. She looked at him and nodded. When her arms came down, slicing the air, a bellowing organ chord filled the cathedral. Red mouthed a silent prayer as if ready to dive, and listened acutely. He felt the chorus take their first beginning breath as he too inhaled before pushing off gently and starting...

Red *became* the music, the beautiful sound, not missing a note, from the "S" to the "I" to the "Lent" to the "Night". He closed his eyes from the magic and splendor of it all. It overwhelmed him, consoled him, lifted his spirit beyond comprehension–singing, so clearly. Suddenly, a surge of gratefulness overcame him and he exclaimed in a rumbling, baritone voice that lilted and boomed, "Round yon virgin mother and child…" His voice was not his own as he praised whatever power that gave him this moment. When the song finished, he remained in a darkened space, his eyes still closed.

The first person he noticed was Olive. She stood stalled, motionless in the front of the choir, her eyes glistening. She blinked. Tears washed down her face. An echoing quiet shrouded the church. And this time he was certain all stares were on him and only him. There was a slight movement in the stunned crowd as a man from a nearby pew sprang up. "Bravissimo," he blurted. Spontaneously, a thunderous applause erupted as the crowd jolted to their feet, clapping wildly, so wildly that the floor shook, the lights flickered.

The Reverend Park pressed through the congregation and pulled Red from the choir. "Just bow," he whispered.

And Red did just that.

❦ ❦ ❦

Author's note:

Every writer should write a Christmas/Hanukkah/Ramadan/Kwansa story. Why? It will make him/her feel good. Yes, I overused adverbs and let the points of view rip. But give the writer a break. It's Christmas. Anyway…

"Red Magill's life started in the minus column," was the inspirational line that first came to me. Little did I know that this line would trouble me through several rewrites. Authors fall in love with sentences, then dig their heels in before letting go. Hours, days can be spent forcing a square peg into a round hole. And even now, three years after its publication, I continue to edit, tweak, the first paragraph of "Birth From A

Star". All so it can follow this first line. I think (fingers crossed), I'm done.

This story is about what we become and how adversity can lead us to a special place.

"Birth From a Star" was first published in Over Coffee.

Shadow Man

What can you glean from a photograph of strangers? How close do they sit, where do they look? And their hands, do they reach out, or hang down uselessly, like unwanted appendages? The shutter clicks in a millisecond and suddenly time stops, memorializing a scene with subtleties not noticed in real time when the picture was taken. However, does the image portray truth or falsehood? Perhaps, like life, it's in the interpretation. There's the photograph and the person who looks at it.

But this isn't a photograph of strangers, unknown, unknowable. The snapshot is of my mother, two sisters and me taken one sunny summer day on the back porch of the cottage. The lake, voluminous and blue, spans behind us. We are all smiling, not huddled together as one might expect for a grown woman and her three young daughters.

I'm leaning along the railing with my arms crossed. I have the vague recollection that I was called up from the beach. I have a plaid bathing suit on with shorts added. My tanned face makes my eyes stand out as well as my teeth. I appear healthy, happy but not a part of the family. I'm behind the others, off to the side, a girl of twelve with other things on her mind–most likely Billie Richard's high school jacket and who he favored for the moment. That summer it was always thoughts of Billie and how to draw his attention away from the other girls.

Michelle is perched on the edge of the glider, next to mother. Her smile is more of a grimace, forced, uncompromising. Her eyes, unreadable, stare directly into the camera. Her arms run the length of her torso and her hands grip the davenport, ready for catapulting. She looks ready to sprint the moment the snapshot is clicked. She wears yellow shorts and a yellow tank top. Her nubby shoulders are about to split through her skin.

Amy, the youngest, is a toddler. Unlike Michelle, she has settled deep into a corner of the davenport. Could this have been her choice, or was she plopped down for the picture? In the tight grasp of her small knuckles is a sucker. Her feet stick out over the cushion. Her eyes are big and round and her mouth is open. She may be laughing or about to take a lick. She is painfully innocent, oblivious to the drama of the moment.

Finally, there's mother, a woman in her prime of fullness, fertility, with luminous eyes and reddened lips. She sits erect and proud in a deep-V buttoned dress with a skinny patent leather belt; her knees are together and slightly turned toward the side, the appropriate way for a lady to sit. Her hair is combed, raked into some type of knob at the nape of her neck. A loose strand hangs down along one side of her face. Her smile is tight, showing no teeth; her industrious fingers are laced, locked uncharacteristically together, on her lap. For a brief moment, she is given a reprieve–nothing to wipe clean, no hair to comb. I draw the picture closer and scan her more carefully. Were there any signs of impending doom? Perhaps an accusing glance, a fleeting downward turn of the lips? But I see nothing of the sort. And I wonder...

What's the picture-taker doing? Deep within our eyes is a mirrored image of him. Would digital technology be able to zoom into our pupils and see the man, our father, who stands in front of us? Is he calm, affable? Giving directions, "Say cheese", "Put your hands down"? Or is he in a rush, with bags packed and the engine running?

How can such critical moments in life go unnoticed and, therefore, unremembered?

Among the three children, I'm considered the lucky one since my memory of him is clearer than theirs. Where I can describe a wholeness, they are left with parts. But as the years passed, even my recollections have lost definition, and I can only recall or choose to recall the most rudimentary of details–he smoked unfiltered cigarettes, was over six feet and smelled of aftershave. And yes, as I'm reminded, he took pictures...

Or at least the one I'm holding now, received less than twenty-four hours ago by registered mail with a short note asking to meet with his daughters for a casual lunch at a hotel restaurant, the perfect venue for extinct lounge lizards and deadbeat dads of thirty years gone by. I'll have to commend him for such an appropriate spot to reacquaint.

Along the white border of the photo is a stamped date, 8-72. The summer before seventh grade, before the move, before the change of schools, before the breakdowns and hysterias, the summer before I became fatherless. On the back, there's writing that appears fresh with clean, even strokes in black ballpoint: *When I last saw you.* And I wonder, to whom is he referring? Me or the group of us. It must be me since the letter was addressed to me, the only one of his daughters who remains unmarried, the one who continues to this day to carry his name, like a saved, useless paperclip in a junk drawer.

I slide the snapshot into my purse pocket and take a fleeting look at myself in the vestibule mirror. Will he recognize me? See something vaguely redundant in how I carry myself or the way I hold my fork? And will these remnants remind him of himself or of his wife, the one he left behind on a beautiful summer day? I cringe knowing whatever we may have in common, our DNA will forever remain an immutable denominator. Still, whatever our shared history is, an even more critical question arises: What shall I call him? Pops?

On the drive to the hotel, I fidget. There's a certain amount of guilt brewing. I've said nothing to my sisters, Michelle, who thinks he's a god, Amy, who craves any detail of him. I tell myself, I'm riding shotgun, preventing an emotional ambush. What does he want anyway? Money, or better yet...a kidney? That would be laughable. Of course, I'd be tested with the hope of being a perfect match, only to say "Sorry, Pops, no can do."

Still, I feel uneasy about the subterfuge, my firm decision to go it alone. Do I want him for myself, like the child I was, the child who hoarded dessert? In a houseful of women with no intervening male presence, I was the selfish one, the controlling one, the one who always got what she wanted. My mother gave me the power after hers was battered and bruised by unanswered prayers and straight vodka. Or perhaps I remain the most discrete, the daughter who, when putting Mother to bed, was privy to secrets no child needed to know. Whatever the reason, my decision is firm.

As I park the car, I wonder if he's watching, staring out from a table near the window or peeping behind a pulled blind in a second-story room. Are his eyes darting across the parking lot, sizing up groups of women who empty from cars? Deep in his chest, is his heart beating like a racehorse, about to burst from running too long? I hope so. And if he, before our meeting, were to have a heart attack secondary to keen anticipation and fathomless guilt...perhaps then there'd be a modicum of forgiveness.

Sharp sunlight glares off car windows assaulting my brain with an ache that is more jarring than painful, a momentary freeze. Advancing, I turn my eyes downward and follow the tips of my shoes. The concrete, its unyielding hardness, is bleak, untenable. Can I do this? What choice do I have? Our meeting is inevitable, like water off a falls. While the past can't be redefined or reconfigured, there are salient points to be made–he must stand accused, he must take responsibility. Not so much for my sake or even my sisters, but for my mother whose life imploded. Suddenly, she was neither widowed nor divorced, but simply husbandless, a vague limbo-like status where future prospects were limited to cheating husbands and mamas' boys who smelled distinctly of mothballs; and where holidays, birthdays, anniversaries began with midmorning Bloody Marys and the interminable (and ultimately senseless) waiting for word by way of a card or letter or collect phone call.

    The hotel lobby is cool and dark. A lingering scent of damp air mingles with a stale citrous smell. Either the carpets were recently cleaned or the conditioning is poorly vented. For a moment, I imagine subatomic torpedo-like particles floating in the air–Legionnaire spores, millions of them. Regardless, I continue onward.

    Monstrous silk-flower arrangements of histrionic lilies in jewel tones not found in nature, are placed strategically in seating areas and against mirrored-walls. The carpet has swirls that loop and spiral, making my eyes roll and my stomach feel queasy. As my pupils adjust, widen like a cat's, I become vigilant to movement and sweep a glance across the reception area. It's critical that I miss no one who may change his mind and skulk away.

    A suited, balding man sits with extended legs in a plush chair. He is alone and reading the newspaper. Over the years, I've often wondered about men of a certain age, men who might be my father. On busses, in restaurants, across crowded rooms, I've fantasized if he, out of desperate curiosity, has followed me. But this man remains absorbed in the sports pages and gives no indication of interest or expectancy.

    To the left, near a corridor entryway, there's a sign on a tripod, *TEA ROOM*, with an arrow. As I stride closer, the sound of clinking dishes becomes clear. Stepping over the threshold, I take a deep breath. It's showtime.

    In a dim vestibule, a dark wooden lectern stands with a posting *Please wait to be seated*. The restaurant proper is a sharp turn to the right beyond an unlit coat check area. According to my watch, I'm fifteen minutes late, fashionably late in most circles, but given the circumstances, generously on time. On a green chalk board, the day's specials are listed. Perhaps, I'll order the lobster. It's the most expensive–time to pay up.

A tall young woman in a crisp white blouse, black slacks, breezes out from the interior. "Welcome to the Tea Room. Table for one?"

"Actually, I meeting someone."

"The name?" she asks as she sways behind the podium.

Name? Do I need to say his name out loud? It seems it should be kept buried where it's been for thirty years, a crumbling bone.

The woman awaits my answer with a disinterested, weak smile. "John," I say feebly, then add, "John Roberts."

A ledger with a list of handwritten names rests on the wood top. She begins to run her finger down the page. I watch carefully, waiting for her glance to stop and get snagged. At the end, she looks up. "Your party's not here yet."

I want to rip the book away from her to check myself. Certainly, he wouldn't stand me up. Would he? How many times in one lifetime can you be sucker-punched by your father?

She pulls a pen from her pocket. "I'll jot his name down and show him in as soon as he arrives. Roberts, right?"

She sounds confident of this eventuality.

"Yes," I say.

Scribbling his name in the margin, she asks, "Would you like to be seated or wait at the bar?"

Drink? I could use a stiff one. "Seated."

Grabbing two leather-bound menus from a compartment below, she says, "This way, please."

I'm settled at a table for two near the window. It would be a pleasant spot if, instead of a parking lot, there were an ocean view. Across the expanse of cars is the highway, and beyond that, the airport. The sky is blue but interrupted. Circling planes leave streams of gray smoke. There is no greenery beyond the glass. It's all a rushed jumble of concrete and metal and sharp edges that, if I look at long enough, will give me a migraine. I open the menu for no other reason than to appear busy. Still, I remain watchful.

A large group takes up several tables arranged end to end. They are talking insurance business, telling war stories of car accidents that are anecdotally amusing. The women in the group are quiet. It's the men who laugh and vie for center stage. Along the perimeter, there appears to be a couple with a college boy in tow. No one speaks. Possibly the empty-nest syndrome is in full swing. Two men (one younger than me, the other older) sit at the bar. A pert young waitress flits across the rug and heads in my direction.

"Hi," she says with a bright smile, "I'm Misty. I'll be your server today." Her glance falls to the other menu. "Would you like a drink while you wait?"

A triple shot of vodka would be my choice at home, but here, in the company of strangers, I say, "A Manhattan on the rocks, please."

"Okey-dokey," she says, and scurries off.

I look at my watch. In five minutes I'll finish the drink then leave. I console myself knowing I have his return address in northern Vermont. From my purse I pull out a pen and appointment book, and flip to a clean page.

Misty returns and sets my drink down on a cocktail napkin. "Compliments from the gentleman at the bar," she says.

My eyes rivet to the area, expecting a vaguely familiar stranger, tall and smiling. But there's only the same two men. I gaze toward the entrance. Had he left, run off, too afraid, embarrassed to finally meet me? I reach for the waitress's arm, "What gentleman?"

"The one on the left," she says and hurries away.

The one on the left is the younger man. He's sitting toward the end of the bar, facing sideways, talking to the older man who's at the very end. When the waitress approaches him, words are exchanged. He then turns in my direction and gives me a wide smile.

He's not unattractive, a salesman-type, suited, short hair, but a bit too beefy for my taste. I suddenly worry if I might know him. Was he one of my indiscretions? There had been some along the way, when I was pathetically desperate for male attention. I return to the blank sheet of paper. Between guzzles, I write, *Hello, bastard child here—*

Without warning, the table rattles. I look up. The salesman-type is sliding into the chair across from me. "Hey, doll."

Instinctively, I reach for my purse and rear back. "Do I know you?"

"Tommy," he says.

I'm suspicious of adult men who have diminutive names or wear their shirts untucked, beach bums. His eyes are very blue and very bloodshot. He could be from the old grove, perhaps somebody's brother or cousin.

"I'm sorry. Have we met?"

"Yes."

"Where?"

"Right here."

"You must be mistaken. I've never been here before."

He leans over, encroaching, smelling of a brewery. "Cute act. Listen, I'm in Room 301, what's your price?"

I'm lightheaded, overheated, and there's a limit. My hand shoots up and I whip it across his face. *Crack.* His head swivels to the side, his smile disintegrates. Immediately he rebounds and seizes the table. I'm certain, he's about to heave the corners up and pummel me down.

"Tommy!" someone yells.

Tommy hisses through clenched teeth. "Whore."

The other man from the bar has crossed the dining room and is putting his hand across Tommy's chest. "Settle down."

Tommy bats the arm away.

"Listen," the older man says, "Get back to the room and get some sleep."

Tommy releases his hands from the table, then shakes out his shoulders.

"We still got to see the Falls," the older man says. "Here, take the keys. Go back to the room. Order a movie or something."

Tommy grabs the keys and rises up. "Whatever," he says before turning around and weaving out the restaurant.

"Listen," says the older man, "I'm sorry. Are you okay?"

"Yes, I think so."

"You'll have to forgive my son. We've been driving all night."

"He's had too much to drink," I say.

"Yes, you're right. Listen, how about lunch?"

"I won't be staying."

"It's just that he was disappointed. We were supposed to meet some family, but they never came."

"Family?"

"His sisters."

We are barely two feet apart. I could easily reach out and feel his skin, follow his features with my fingertips like someone blind. But I only look.

For a man of sixty-two, he has aged poorly. Clusters of broken spider veins spread across his pasty cheeks, unkempt hairs sprout from his ears, nose. But it's his eyes that catch my breath—they are recessed and definitively gray with the tiniest flecks of green and yellow, something I now recall. "You'll have to excuse me," I say.

Moments later, I've boxed myself into the corner stall of the ladies room. I want the electricity to go out, make me invisible. I shut my eyes. Darkness envelops me, wraps me in comfort. Here, there are no shadows, nothing to assault or evade me. I gain strength and open my eyes. The piercing light hurts, but after a few minutes I'll hardly notice.

I walk out the lavatory and step onto the spongy carpet of the restaurant. He remains at the bar. I feel a strong magnetic pull, both intuitive and potent, but it's not in his direction. In a few short steps, I pivot and exit, first from the restaurant, then from the hotel.

Stepping off the curb, a slight breeze brushes against my skin. The distant traffic sounds like waves. Once in the car, I turn the key and the engine catches. Pumping up the volume, I shift into drive and drill my foot onto the gas pedal. With the reverberating rev of pistons, I swerve into the road.

Suddenly the day turns glorious.

❊   ❊   ❊

Author's note:

The Ten Commandments fail to include "Do Not Abuse or Neglect Your Children". If every child was loved and cared for, the world would be a very different place. Abandonment of a child is criminal, its long term effects devastating.

On TV talk shows, parent/child reunions have become commonplace. The breast-pounding parent bleats "mea culpas" while citing extenuating circumstances. The child, hardwired to love his parent no matter what, is an open wound. Not surprising, happy endings are rare.

Caroline, the unnamed protagonist in "Shadow Man", is given an option: to leave or to stay. A parallel moment arises, similar to a past summer day. Only this time, there's a critical difference–the power is hers.

The Smuggler

Figuring the odds was something Patrick did. It forced him to take a bird's eye view of a situation and do some quick calculating.

So on his way to Toronto, locked amid a clot of jagged-moving traffic at the Canadian border, he wondered about the probabilities. How many vehicles around him were loaded down with contraband? Would a guestimate of five percent be reasonable? And of those, how many would be caught? One out of four?

As Patrick crept forward to the customs booth, he relaxed. While he had nothing illegal heading out of the country, he would have his personal stash of Cuban cigars upon reentry. But that was hardly his concern now. After answering the few familiar questions, he sped off onto the Queen E, looking forward to his bimonthly visit.

Patrick loved Toronto. It was a great town, sort of like the Big Apple on chill pills and judging by the Toronto Star, the odds of getting murdered on the street remained significantly less than in an American city a quarter of its size. There he'd buy a box of cigarros at Julio's, check out the bookstores, and eat at a few of his favorite restaurants.

So when Patrick stopped by The Blue Room for an early lunch, he was surprised to see Delia, his old girlfriend. Now, what were the odds of that?

Before they split, Delia had come with him on other visits. They had hung out for three years, but when she heard wedding bells and

Patrick didn't, they found themselves at an impasse and called it quits.

Anyway, Delia was sitting in a corner booth. At first Patrick thought she was a look alike. He didn't understand it, but as he got older he saw more similarities between people than he used to. It was funny how he noticed her. She was wearing a yellow coat, the color of a banana, bright and distracting. Patrick thought to himself, caution, stay away. He didn't like showy women, so vigilant for attention. However, there was that familiarity, the curve of her cheek, and of course she was in *their* spot. He waited until she spoke to the waitress, and bingo, her low husky voice brought back a flood of candlelight memories.

Patrick considered walking right out, taking his leave, but heck they had parted on good terms and she was a good sport. He collected his newspaper, cup of coffee, and sidled up next to her.

"This seat taken?" he asked.

Surprise registered on her face. She crooked her head to one side and her eyebrows rose.

"Patrick?" she asked vaguely.

For a brief moment, he had an uneasy feeling. Sure his hair was grayer and he had put on a few pounds but could he have aged beyond recognition? In any event, not to be outdone, he answered, "Del?"

Her lips, red and shiny, parted in a wide smile. "How are you?"

Patrick slid onto the bench. "Great. Yourself?"

"Pretty good."

Yeah, and she looked fine too. Her hair was blonder than he remembered and her sweater fit great. "So what brings you to Toronto?"

"Shopping. My sister's getting married, and I want to get her something special."

"Dana's found a man? Gainfully employed, I hope."

Delia took a deep breath. "You never change, do you?"

Less than thirty seconds into a conversation, and Patrick had put his foot in his mouth. Okay, it wasn't the best opener. He needed a rebound. "Hey, I'm joking."

"Sure you are."

"What can I get you? Wanna sandwich, dessert?"

"It's eleven o'clock in the morning."

He checked his watch. "Right. How about an omelet or one of those flaky things?"

"A croissant?"

"Yeah. You used to like those."

Del looked at him intently. Their eyes locked. Croissants were always in the continental breakfasts they had ordered in hotels, and suddenly Patrick wondered if there was a chance of a replay.

"No thank you," she finally answered.

"You here for the day?"

"Yeah. Yourself?"

"Heading back home tomorrow. Got a room at the Royal York."

He scanned her face for some spark, some acknowledgment of their shared history.

A glimmer flashed in her eyes, before she quickly regrouped. "You always gave interesting presents. Got any ideas for a wedding gift?"

Patrick had plenty of ideas, and if he played his cards right maybe he could parlay a little romance.

"How about a cloisonné piece?" he suggested.

"What's that?"

"Chinese enamel work, beautiful stuff. Probably find some in Chinatown."

"Oh, I don't feel comfortable going there by myself."

Patrick lowered his voice. "Not comfortable? What about the little present I gave you for your birthday?"

She glanced around, then added with a naughty smile. "THAT wasn't little. Besides it could get me arrested."

Patrick smiled, amused by Del's quick repartee and double entendre.

"Listen, I got nothing planned. I can take you," he said.

"You sure?"

Her eyes were bluer than he remembered. "Of course I'm sure."

They shopped for the rest of the day, first to Chinatown, then up on Bloor. Before long they held hands, and once she found the perfect gift, an antique silver tea set, Patrick insisted they go for a bite. He ordered wine, her weakness, and by nine that evening the couple revisited their past in Room 357 at the Royal York. The following morning, they parted.

On the way back home, Patrick felt like he had a month's vacation. Del was mighty okay in his book.

At the border, he was asked to pull over and wait inside. His luck had run out and he'd probably have to hand over the Cuban cigars. Still, it was a small inconvenience that wasn't going to ruin his mood. Unruffled, he watched as two border patrolmen descended onto his car.

Ten minutes later an officer approached him. "Mr. McCarthy, you got a permit for this?"

"For a couple of cigars?" Patrick said without much thought.

The patrolman hoisted the evidence bag to Patrick's face. "No, for an Arcadia automatic with hollow-points."

Its blue finish and checkered walnut handle was vaguely familiar. "That wasn't in my car."

"It was under the front passenger seat."

Patrick's glance ricocheted from the officer to beyond the plate glass windows where a car with a blond-haired driver pulled onto the shoulder.

Suddenly, the pieces fell into place. The bedroom special had been his last gift to her. As the cuffs snapped behind his back, Del blew him a kiss then sped away.

Patrick shook his head. For all his calculations, he hadn't figured the odds of meeting a thwarted lover.

❦   ❦   ❦

Author's note:

Retribution rears its ugly head again. Alas, what's a girl to do? Perhaps, for those commitment phobic men who refuse to walk down the aisle, having a full body search would suffice. (Spread 'em.)

But, seriously, this is only a story, a little ditty to amuse readers as they await being called for their dental cleaning.

Disclaimer: Author takes no responsibility for any actions a thwarted lover may take. Author denies ever having taken such action. Author asserts that any semblance to person or persons alive, dead, or in suspended animation, is purely coincidental.

"The Smuggler" was first published in Cenotaph.

Moose

At the wedding reception *Marcy & Dale Forever* had been written across the cocktail napkins, but forever fell a tad short, and they split before their tenth anniversary. It was a civilized break-up, no recriminations of who left the toilet seat up or down, no blaming of who forgot whose birthday. They simply lounged on Adirondack chairs one summer evening on their deck, not a season old, and discussed the situation. Dale began with what most errant husbands tell their soon-to-be ex-wives. "I love you, but I'm not in love with you."

Marcy took the news better than most. She sipped her vodka tonic, popped a few olives in her mouth and said, "Will you be taking Moose?" He answered probably not since he was downsizing to an apartment, hers, the woman he was in love with. And it was at this defining moment that Marcy stood up and sternly said, with no room for debate, "You wanted him, he's yours," leaving Dale to ponder, in the elongated shadows of a setting sun, a serious dilemma– Laurene, the woman he was in love with, was a cat person. Moose wasn't.

Moose, a 150 lb., four-year-old Newfoundland had soulful eyes, deeply rich and chocolate brown, that belied the animal's true nature. While the dog appeared oafish and good humored (he rarely barked, or jumped, or bared his teeth), unlike most dogs his breed, he had a singularly narcissistic nature, complemented by a slew of bad habits. And so, before Dale called Laurene to tell her the good news, he telephoned Kareem's Dog Obedience School and enrolled

Moose in an intensive three-week behavior modification program that cost six hundred dollars, which according to the proprietor, was one-hundred percent guaranteed.

The class at Kareem's was small, only two other dogs with their owners. A Doberman with a sleek coat, the color of wet pavement at night, was muzzled and restless, as he pulled and twisted his lead, tangling up his master's legs. A Chihuahua yapped incessantly in the crook of an older woman's arm. Moose dropped to the floor and yawned. Disclosure followed.

The Chihuahua, Buffy, terribly bloated, with buggy, protruding eyes, teetered on legs as scrawny as popsicle sticks. Not only was the animal hugely disproportionate, but as Dale learned, it had a nasty habit of snapping at small children, specifically bolting upright and lunging for their noses.

Ruben, the 9-month-old, skittish Doberman, came from a pedigree line of insomniacs prone to suspected hallucinations (he stalked and growled for reasons unknown). Dale deduced generations of inbreeding probably caused a proliferation of recessive genes that left the animal incapable of dealing with stimuli. It was as if his nervous system were tightly strung with an inordinate amount of neurons, like an overloaded plug in a rented room, which flooded his brain with near lethal doses of electrical current. What else could explain the flash in his eyes, his constant vigilance?

Dale was encouraged. Even though Moose was gangly, he was otherwise proportional, calm and, from all appearances, a concrete thinker. Clearly a prince whose problems paled to these two. Dale, like a proud father in a child's waiting room, reached down and patted Moose's head. "Good boy." Moose acknowledged his master's gesture by passing gas, a silent bomb that filled the room.

When Dale was asked what brought him and Moose to class, the other owners looked at him expectantly, solemnly, as if they all were on a sinking ship. Dale's mind locked. He wanted to be discrete, tasteful. "Moose is really quite good. A tad lazy perhaps but…well, he can be a bit stubborn when it comes to…ah…personal hygiene."

Eyebrows rose.

The trainer, a woman in overalls and a ponytail, asked, "Could you be more specific?"

"He has accidents."

Commiserative nods followed.

"And how old is Moose?"

Dale lied. "Around a year."

"That old? How have you been managing?"

Dale wondered that himself. But of course he wasn't the one doing the managing. He thought about the steps Marcy had taken.

"He's in a restricted area during the day. You know, where there are hard surfaces like the basement, garage."

"And at night?"

"Stays mostly in the kitchen."

"I see," said the trainer. "Are there any other concerns?"

Concerns? What was this, group therapy? Dogs Anonymous? Dale refused to go into further detail. "That's about it."

"Has Moose ever been crated?"

"I'm not sure what you mean."

"Kept in a cage, "said Buffy's mother.

"No, of course not," Dale answered.

"Well then, that's where we'll start," said the trainer.

An hour and one hundred and ten dollars later, Dale and Moose headed home with very specific directions and a very large crate. Moose's lifestyle was about to change. At a stop light, Dale reached over and scratched Moose behind his ears. "Times are a'changin buddy." He then thought about Laurene and her silky thighs.

The weeks following Dale and Moose's trek to Kareem's were emotionally trying but productive. Since Dale had to postpone his move into Laurene's until Moose's behavior was more under control, he relocated into the spare room. Marcy, when home, slammed around in the kitchen and left sticky notes on those things she intended to keep, which pretty much included everything but the rowing machine, vaporizer, and of course Moose. Dale wasn't about to argue.

On the upside, Moose progressed beautifully. That very night after class, he slept in the crate and woke up clean and dry. Dale wanted to tell Marcy, it was just a matter of scheduling, consistency and showing who's boss. Moose ate one meal per day and was taken out once in the morning and twice in the evening. The rest of the time, he was confined. Within weeks, Moose morphed into a model pet, and all systems were go.

Laurene lived in a second floor apartment with vaulted ceilings and sky lights. Throughout the day and depending on the angle of the sun, diffused light would cast soft shadows onto the walls and upholstered furniture, all buff-colored. Often following an afternoon romp, Dale, reluctant to leave, had lingered while Laurene prepared dinner amid the classical strains of Bach and the sweet scent of vanilla candles. As Dale now climbed the carpeted stairs with the new and improved Moose (recently bathed in aromatics at Kareem's), he was ebullient. The months of wrangling two women were now over and he could finally be immersed in the sex and serenity of Laurene.

At the door to her apartment, Dale knocked then squared his shoulders.

"Be there in a sec," Laurene called out.

Dale pulled Moose's leash to have him sit. Once on his haunches, Moose looked at Dale expectantly, waiting for a treat. Dale put his fingers to his lips and shh-ed.

A moment later, Laurene, in a tight, white T-shirt and faded jeans, opened the door. As her glance fell to the dog, her wide, bright smile froze. "So this is Moose."

At hearing his voice, Moose stood on all fours and pitched forward, aiming his nose inches from her crotch. She reared back. "My, he's big."

Dale shortened the leash by looping it around his wrist. He then tugged discretely. "Yeah, this is my baby."

Laurene opened the door wide, allowing enough room for a three-man moving crew and refrigerator.

Dale and Moose crossed the threshold and entered. Halfway into the living room, Moose stopped dead. Asleep on the couch in the folds of a tapestry throw were Curly and Moe, Laurene's two Persian cats.

Dale tightened his grip. "Be good, Moose."

Moe, a fat ball of tan fur, lazily lifted her lids. Upon seeing Moose, her eyes popped open. Immediately, she catapulted from her spot and dove beneath the couch. Curly, having been jostled by Moe's movement, raised her head, pulled her ears back and screeched. Laurene rushed to the couch.

Dale pushed hard on Moose's back. "Down, boy," he said sternly. In response, Moose collapsed to a prone position and panted. Saliva dripped from his mouth.

Laurene gathered Curly in her arms. "Pretty kitty, don't be afraid," she cooed. The cat flailed at her chest, trying to escape.

Dale reached over to pat Curly's head. The little czarina hissed. He backed off and said, "I know Moose is big and a bit intimidating but he wouldn't hurt a fly. Pet him. You'll see."

"I have my hands full," she said with a hint of irritation.

"Darn kids," Dale said sheepishly.

Laurene didn't seem amused and began pacing, holding the cat as if it were a crying baby.

"Honey, with time they'll get along. Besides, once the house is sold, we can start looking for a bigger place."

Laurene's shoulder's loosened. She walked around the room keeping a watchful eye on Moose then settled into the couch. "But what are we going to do till then?"

Dale had it figured out. "I'll set the crate up in the spare bedroom. It'll be out of the way and the cats can still have the run of the house, and maybe (he wanted to sound tentative, but it was hardly negotiable) after I get home from work, we can let him out and have them get acclimated to one another."

As Dale spoke, Laurene stroked the underside of Curly's chin. "When will we be able to move into a house?"

"I don't know, maybe six months."

"Six months!"

"Well, it's hard to say. But, heck, if you like, we could start looking now and buy on contingency."

Her face seemed to soften, the downward corners of her lips relaxed and she made eye contact.

He continued, "In fact there's no reason why we can't start looking this weekend. Maybe take a drive and see what's available."

Stroking Curly's fur, she asked, "Really? We could do that?"

"Sure. Why not? Where would you like to live?"

"The suburbs, of course. But which one? And I suppose we should consider the schools."

"Schools?"

"Just in case," she said in a teasing tone.

Dale smiled. They hadn't discussed children, but then they never did too much talking.

Curly's eyes were half-closed. In less than ten minutes, familial bliss seemed well within reach. Dale relaxed his grip on the lease and Moose's head dropped to the floor.

"There's a beautiful development off Route 75. How much do you think we'll be able to afford?" she asked.

"I'd have to figure that out."

"They're around two fifty."

Two hundred and fifty thousand! Had houses gone up that much?

Laurene continued. "Of course, a house is an investment. When you think of what you get, three baths, a two-car garage with everything brand-new, it's really quite reasonable. And guess what else? Instead of electric street lights, there are gas lanterns and the roads have French names. Dale, it's so quaint."

"French, huh?"

"Yeah, like Arc de Triumph and Champs de something-or-other."

Laurene's eyes were shining now, full of life.

"Sounds elegant," Dale commented, even though he thought the la-de-dah names were a marketing ploy for frustrated Francophiles, who, like most Americans, preferred the knock-off to the original.

"No harm in looking. Right?"

She beamed. "Right."

"So when would you like to go?"

"Tomorrow after breakfast?"

"Works for me."

She glanced down at Moose, whose head rested on his paws. "He really is quite tame, isn't he? Not like a bear at all."

"Yeah, he's terrific, You'll see. So, do you think Moe will be all right?" he asked, more out of reciprocal kindness than true concern.

"Don't worry. She's timid with everyone. And look at Curly, why she's already fallen asleep. Can't be that upset."

"It's official then, we're a blended family," Dale said, feeling relieved.

"Yes, I suppose you're right. But then you always are," she said in a velvety, throaty voice. "Oh, I almost forgot. I have a cheesecake in the oven. I'll put Curly in my bedroom for now. Would you like something to drink?"

"Sure."

Laurene got up from the couch with Curly in her arms. On the way out, she bent down and pecked Dale on the cheek. The scent of her body wash reminded him of the foamy showers they had taken and how the suds had clung then ran down her slick body.

Alone with Moose, Dale nudged his foot into the animal's fleshy side. Moose raised his head.

"What up, dawg?" Dale said.

Moose's tail thumped on the rug.

"Nice crib, huh?"

Moose stared expectantly into Dale's eyes.

"I take that as a yes," Dale responded.

In the background, Laurene could be heard in the kitchen. The oven door closed and water ran from the tap.

"Need any help?" he yelled.

"No everything's under control."

Looking around, Dale noticed that the dinette table was set with linens, fresh flowers and tapered candles.

"Pretty fancy table. Are you expecting company?" he called out.

"I'm making a special dinner for us. All your favorites," she said as she entered the room with a glass of red wine.

Sitting on the arm of the chair, she handed him the drink.

After he took a sip, she reached out. "Can I have a taste?"

He handed her the glass, but she set it on the coffee table. Bending toward him, she said, "This kind of taste." She then nibbled his lip and explored his mouth with her tongue. "Mmm," she said, then whispered in his ear. "I'm feeling naughty."

"Naughty is good," Dale murmured.

Laurene ran her hand over his chest, then unbuckled his belt and slipped her hand beneath. With each stroke, he swelled harder. Distracted, Dale let go of the leash.

For so many months, sandwiched between stolen moments, Dale's sexuality had been programmed to respond quickly. Not yet accustomed to the limitless span of hours, days, he wanted to take her fast. Grabbing her wrist, he pulled her hand away. "Straddle me," he said.

Fully dressed, she complied and faced him on the chair. He yanked her T-shirt off and fumbled with her bra. Topless, she arched her back and he took a nipple into his mouth. She moaned. Fiddling with her jeans, she suddenly lurched forward, ramming into his face. "Oh my god! Something's crawling on me."

Dale half-stunned, craned his neck to see. "What the—" he said and began to laugh. Moose had gotten up and was standing directly behind Laurene. Had he poked his nose into her back? "He must like you."

"That's not funny, Dale."

Putting his arms around her, she collapsed into him.

"You're right. Sorry. Maybe he thinks you're attacking me."

She shivered. "Why is he staring? Get him away."

"Down, Moose," Dale said firmly.

Immediately, the dog fell to the floor.

"See, there's nothing to worry about," he said as he nuzzled into her, wanting to pick up where he left off.

Laurene hoisted herself off him. "I can't do this. You've got to put him in his crate."

"It's in the trunk," he said lamely, hoping for few moments to thrust and finish up. But she already was slipping into her T-shirt.

"All right. It shouldn't take long. Bookmark our spot." He stood and zipped his pants. "Where can I leave Moose?"

She looked askance at the animal. "Will he be okay where he is?"

"Yeah, this is probably the best spot. If I put him in the bedroom, he may scratch the door. You can keep an eye on him and he won't get lonely. Can you manage?"

"I suppose. You won't be long, will you?"

"Heck, no. A couple of minutes. Tops."

"Will he stay lying down?"

Dale scanned the room, then considered his chair. "Here, I'll secure the leash to the bottom of the chair leg. As long as he's tied up, he won't move."

"You sure?"

"Scouts honor thanks to Kareem's Obedience School. Moose is a graduate, you know."

A small smile creased her lips. "Bachelor's?"

"Master's, actually."

"That's reassuring. While you're doing that, I'll get the room ready."

On his way out, Dale stopped, wrapped his arms around Laurene's waist and kissed her neck. She swayed into him and whispered, "Hurry."

Taking two steps at a time, Dale jettisoned down the flight of stairs, flew out the front door and ran to the car. The metal mesh crate, partially disassembled and folded, needed wrangling before freeing it from the trunk. He then grabbed the metal floor insert and jostled each item under his arms. Climbing the porch stairs, he stopped, not once but twice. The cumbersome load kept slipping. At the front entry, with his arms full, he kicked the door open. Banging through the doorway, knocking and scraping the door jamb, he froze. Moe, Laurene's cat, cowered in a dark corner of the vestibule, suddenly bolted between his legs and bounded off the porch. "Damn," Dale said under his breath. Had he left the upstairs door opened? The crate clattered to the floor as he dropped everything and sprung after the cat.

For a lazy ball of fur, the darn thing was on fire. After barreling down the steps, she hair-pinned deep into a cavernous overhang of bushes. Dale hit the ground and peered through brambles and spider webs. Hunched along the concrete foundation, Moe looked at him with dark saucers-like eyes and hissed. Dale inched toward the cat, digging his elbows into the gritty dirt. Branches poked and scraped his face as he crawled. Within reach, he said, "Nice kitty." The cat's glance parried left and right as Dale dove forward with a grasping hand. A fleeting tail slipped through his fingers. From his perspective on the ground, he saw the cat bound into the open and spring across the side lawn. Dale retreated from the tangle of brush. Slapping off the dirt from his knees and elbows, Dale vowed to catch the pisser and wring its neck. But as he turned the corner of the house, the search and destroy mission was over. Twenty feet above in a sugar maple, Moe was continuing her ascent.

Climbing the stairs, wrangling the crate, Dale considered his apology. Yes, he probably left the door ajar, and yes, he was sorry. The next step was to call 911, which he would do. As far as continuing their romantic interlude. Well, that would take some diplomacy and a few drinks.

At the landing to her apartment, the door was wide open. Had he been that absent-minded? Entering the hall and passing into the living room, an uneasy feeling overcame him—the chair that had pinned down Moose's leash was toppled over. Quickly scanning the area, his stomach sank. Puddled on the floor was the tablecloth amid a tangled mess of broken dishes and scattered flowers. Moose! He must have been chasing Moe.

"Laurene?" Dale called out.

A whimpering came from the kitchen. He rushed to the doorway and stopped dead.

Moose was humping wildly to something prone on the floor. Beneath his tail, were Laurene's slippered feet. "My God," he exhaled. "Moose, heel," he screamed. But the dog was on automatic pilot.

Reeling across the floor, he lunged for the animal's neck. The dog's strength was yeoman. Dale head-locked Moose and twisted his head to the side forcing the animal down. With the dog hauled off, Dale got a glimpse of Laurene. Her face was dazed and contorted.

"You all right?" he said with Moose still clutched in a bear hug.

She sat up and took a deep breath. Looking over at Moose, she rumbled, seething with anger, "Get him out of here."

Dale scurried to his feet and retrieved Moose's lead. "I'll take him into the bedroom."

"Like hell! Get him out of this apartment."

"Out of the apartment? But—"

"There's no way I'm living with that…that animal!"

"But we agreed to—"

"Listen, he not only attacked Moe and trashed my house, but he fucking molested me, Dale."

"Molested you. Well, isn't that sort of, umm…"

"Of umm what?"

"An exaggeration."

She was standing now, pointing to a wet spot on her jeans. "This is no exaggeration!"

"It's just that we never got around to having him fixed. He gets frisky sometimes. Listen, I'll call the vet and make an appointment."

"That dog is demented. It's either him or me, Dale. Your call."

"You're upset. I realize that. Now let me get him in his cr—"

"Get Out!" she bellowed.

"Okay, settle down. Now about Moe."

"What about Moe?"

"She's up a tree."

With no warning, Laurene grabbed a kitchen knife and lunged for Moose. "You mother fu—"

Plunging to meet her advance, mild-mannered Moose, bared his teeth and snapped at the knife. Dale gripped the lead with two hands and yanked hard. "Laurene, you're being unreasonable."

Her face tightened. Suddenly she was an old hag, thin-lipped and spitting mean. "How dare you!"

"Fine, we're going," Dale said, grasping Moose's collar to haul him away.

As the two sprung from the kitchen, a pot careened past Dale's ear and smashed into a wall. Fearing bodily harm if he were to make another trip, Moose's crate was left behind.

❈ ❈ ❈

Several hours later, Dale and Moose registered in a motel thirty miles east of the city off the interstate. They had tried to return home, but Marcy had the locks changed. Sleepy Tyme wasn't a bad place, a bit musty, but there was plenty of land (an abandoned railroad track ran the length of the property)to take walks. The owner was amenable to Moose as long as he didn't bark. The room had three double beds, cable and a complimentary single pack of instant coffee.

The first night they picked up a pizza and stopped for beer. In the supermarket, Dale considered buying dog food but decided against it–cans would require an opener, a dish, spoon, and the dry stuff would stink up the room. It was then that Dale figured that they'd both eat take-out until either Laurene or Marcy returned his calls.

After three weeks, neither did. Faced with unwanted, unintended bachelorhood, Dale stopped shaving and wore wrinkled clothes to work–the beginning of his downward spiral. Weeks of drinking too much, eating garbage, and slamming the ham followed. But a few days before Thanksgiving, Dale had an epiphany. It wasn't about him specifically, or Laurene, or Marcy. It was about Moose.

The realization came on a Saturday afternoon during a Notre Dame football game. He and Moose were lying on the double bed closest to the television, eating potato chips (his were regular, Moose's were barbecue) when Dale said something about needing a drink. Moose lumbered off to the bathroom where a pack of ice was melting in the tub, and retrieved what was left of a six pack. Crawling back onto the bed, the dog dropped the two cans that were still connected to the plastic web. Dale forgot about the impending field goal, grabbed Moose's face and looked deeply into the animal's eyes. "What's up with you?" he said. "Not only are you not crapping or humping or passing gas, but you're getting my beer?" Moose, of course, hadn't yet learned to talk but he did wag his tail. It was then the epiphany occurred. It had to do with being restricted and living in a crate.

The next day, Dale and Moose moved into an apartment.

🍁   🍁   🍁

Author's note:

I rarely write about myself–bor-ring. But in the case of "Moose", I decided to share.

I was in my early twenties at the time, dateless, boyfriend-less with no prospects when Ralph, the local newfie, paid a visit. Actually it wasn't me he wanted to see (euphemism), but Pearl, my black lab, who happened to be in heat.

It was Sunday morning and I had my whites on. (At the time I worked as a Nurse's aide.) Ralph had been camped on my front porch for a week, waiting tenaciously for a chance to win Pearl's heart(euphemism). After I locked the front door and stumbled over his tail I said, "Ralph, go home, get some sleep." He pleaded to me with mournful brown eyes.

I continued to my car, put the key in the door and BAM, on hinds legs, Ralph plastered his body against mine and began to get what he had come for. Well, not quite. Anyway...

Moose is the most loving character in this story, just as pets so often are.

"Moose" was first published in The Southern Cross Review.

Elsie's Disappearance

When Elsie disappeared, rumors flew that she had run off with her still-married boyfriend, Henry. But when Henry showed up at the Landmark for his daily senior citizen lunch, stating that he hadn't seen Elsie since the Friday before, well, that theory was scratched, leaving the daunting question: When a seventy-three-year-old woman ended up missing, what was someone to think? One thing for sure, certainly not that she was in Oahu having a Mai Tai.

What the police found after the mailman alerted them to Elsie's ungathered mail, was a house in disarray. Drawers in the kitchen and bedroom were emptied, and the mattress was pulled from her bed. A man's size-twelve Nike sneaker print was left everywhere along with an unidentifiable fingerprint on a Snapple bottle found in a dusty corner of the living room. In a rear utility room, shattered glass from a broken window covered the carpet. Had anyone seen or heard anything?

Turned out that Kirsten Mae, a high school student and Elsie's next door neighbor, was the only person in close proximity to the event in question (her parents having gone out of town to a wedding) and she was subsequently questioned by the police.

Kirsten had little information to pass along–no screams, no gunshots, no sounds of breaking glass. After the police left, she ran upstairs to her room and slammed the door, causing a snapshot that was tacked on the wall to fall. Kirsten picked it up, smoothed her fingers over the photograph of a white-haired woman, her adopted grandmother, and tried settling her heart down.

Three weeks after Elsie's disappearance, a most noteworthy discovery was made. Elsie's life insurance policy had Kirsten's name jotted down as beneficiary. It had been signed three years previous and was for one million dollars. Immediately, a request was made for Kirsten to take a lie detector test.

After the warm up inquiries of the date, time of the month, color of the sky, the critical questions began: "Do you know anything about Elsie Higgins' disappearance?"

"Anything?" she asked.

"Answer yes or no."

"Well, yes."

The examiner stopped the machine. "What do you know?"

She fiddled with her hands. "I know lots of things about her disappearance. It was in the news. The day it may have happened, the condition of her home—"

The examiner nodded briskly. "I see, okay. Forget that question. We'll start again."

He turned on the machine. "Are you involved with Elsie Higgins' disappearance?"

Kirsten figured this would come up. "Yes," she answered.

Again, he shut the machine off. "How are you involved?"

"Well, that's why I'm here. I've been involved from the beginning since I live next door."

The man held up his hand to quiet her. He then clicked the machine back on. "Did you or anyone you know kidnap Elsie Higgins?"

"No."

"Did you or anyone you know kill Elsie Higgins?"

"No."

And that was the end of that.

Upon returning home, Kirsten breathed deeply. The worst was over, no more waiting for the other shoe to fall. After listening for her parents and hearing their voices rumbling downstairs, she tiptoed into her closet and pulled a message beeper from beneath the floorboards. She punched in three words *fish, blood, teeth*. And the second leg of the journey began.

Approximately ten days after Kirsten sent her cryptic message, a gruesome discovery was found. Along an uninhabited stretch of ocean, north of Palm Beach, a large, unhinged cooler floated ashore. It was empty but dried blood smears appeared along the rim. A few days later, two miles away, a blood soaked housedress and set of false teeth were found tangled among some brush. Elsie Higgins' body was never found, perhaps sharks had gotten to it. But the DNA was hers, as was the dress, as was the set of dentures. Shortly after that, Elsie was pronounced dead and her estate probated, making Kirsten a very wealthy young woman.

Kirsten had bought the man's sneakers at the local Goodwill second-hand store. As for the Snapple, the fingerprints were of a check out clerk. She had broken Elsie's window with a crow bar and entered the house wearing the sneakers and some rubber gloves from a hair dying kit. After emptying the drawers for no particular reason, she then walked out the front door and returned home.

Two years later, Kirsten drove to Brown University in her brand-new BMW. One afternoon her sorority sister called her to the phone.

"Hello, Kirsten," a familiar voice said.

Kirsten's heart beat wildly.

"So we did it."

"Yes, we did," Kirsten agreed.

"I won't keep you but I will be needing the money."

"Of course. Shall I send it by mail?"

"Yes. Registered mail, a cashier's check."

"Okay." Kirsten reached for a pen. "How should I address it?"

"Pat Mullins, 73 Peony. Take care of yourself."

Kirsten did as she was told, keeping her remaining share of two hundred thousand. At the post office, she approached the clerk and asked, "Excuse me, what's the zip code for Oahu, Hawaii?"

※　　　※　　　※

Author's note:

Tuition to Ivy League schools is often paid by grandparents. Ergo, Elsie had to be creative.

I like mysteries. I like reading them. I like writing them. I like putting a hook into the readers mouth and pulling on the line, first one way, then another. But sometimes the reader is smarter than me and isn't snagged. Congratulations. But I'll get you next time.

"Elsie's Disappearance" was first published in Cenotaph.

A Father's Love

My earliest memory was at the kitchen table, in the morning, while I made Rice Krispies. I had to stand on the chair to pour the milk (partly missing the bowl) and when I sat back down, puddles of milk and cereal dotted the table from the overflow. Between mouthfuls, I blew on the scattered rice that looked like little boats sailing away. And with my finger, I connected the puddles, making rivers, and when the spilt milk was too thin to spread I'd spoon some extra from my bowl.

Out of nowhere came Dad. At first, I thought, he was going to holler, but he grinned and lifted me high off the chair. "How's my little queenie," he said. He then carried me to the living room and sat me on his lap. He kissed my forehead, scratching my cheek with his face, and it tickled. But after a while I wanted to get up. Daisy was crying in another room. He didn't seem to notice, and with his arms locked around me, he said, "Daddy's got to sleep."

There were many times he didn't come home at night and we were left alone. And every morning, before going downstairs, I'd peek in his room to see if there was a mountain in his bed. It wasn't a problem though, because I knew how to take care of Daisy.

Then one night I woke up to a loud noise. At first I thought it was thunder. I curled up along the wall on the far side of the bed with a blanket nearly covering my head and waited for a flash of lightning. Instead another sound pounded the walls and shook the room. It came from under me somewhere. I jumped up and bolted to the window. That's when I saw the tops of two men throwing themselves against the back door. I got scared like never before. Shrieking out into the hall, I ran to Dad's room and threw myself into his half-opened bedroom door. I blinked once, twice, wishing what I saw away—the bed was flat.

The house shook again with a loud cracking noise. I rushed to Daisy's room, gathered her the best I could and dashed up the attic stairs.

I stood on the top landing, stuck, afraid to move. Daisy whimpered and I covered her mouth with my hand. I couldn't hear any more thuds and for a second I thought everything was over. But heavy footsteps and gruff low voices echoed up the stairwell. They were in the house.

"We're going to play Hide and Seek," I whispered to Daisy. She looked at me wide-eyed. My heart pounded but I knew I was good at this game, in fact I was the best—one time I hid in a wastepaper basket with sheets on top of me.

The attic was dark. Still I could tell from the outlines of things that on the other side of some boxes, two mattresses leaned against the wall. It was a perfect spot. I slid sideways between the cartons and jammed my shoulder into the middle seam. It separated. I held Daisy tight and I tucked in backwards, pushing as hard as I could with my feet until total blackness and padding wrapped around us. Once inside I let my body slide down to the floor. We crunched up and I put my finger to my mouth with a "sh."

They were on the second floor now. Something crashed. A few seconds later, footsteps, the loudest I ever heard, came up the attic stairs. It became very quiet and a flash of light sparked by the tiny opening we had just made.

"Junk," a man said.

"This whole place is junk. Let's get outta here," said another, and they charged back down. The attic door slammed.

The next thing I heard was Dad's voice screaming my name. A triangle of sunlight shined in between the mattresses. "Here we are!" I yelled. But my voice was swallowed up by the thick padded walls. I shoved Daisy in front of me, forcing her ahead. Dad called me again but he was sounding further away. Desperate he would leave, I pushed Daisy so hard she popped out and fell flattened on the attic floor. I clawed over her and sped down the stairs.

When Dad saw me, he ran and scooped me up, lifting me as high as I had ever been. He spun me around so fast my legs flew behind me. I criss-crossed my arms around his neck and closed my eyes tight. "Where's Daisy?" he asked. But I wouldn't let go. He asked me again and we tore up to the attic.

He carried us around all day. It was better than being on any ride, especially when we went up and down the stairs. I told him everything and he promised he would never leave us alone again. The police came with sirens. Dad told them we were all asleep when it happened. He told me he had to say that so he wouldn't go to jail. He also said I was very brave and the best daughter he could ask for.

When they came over to fix the door, they put in a metal one with screws as long as my finger. Still, it didn't seem enough to stop someone from breaking in.

After that Daisy and I went to sleep in his room and he slept on the couch—just in case. This went on for a while until Daisy wet the bed. Eventually, we ended up in our own rooms and things got back to normal.

I helped around the house the best I could. He taught me how to scramble eggs and make toast and I learned to set the table and pour beer without spilling any. When he had his friends over to play cards, I'd make sure the bowls were filled with potato chips and I'd take away the empty bottles and get cold ones from the fridge. It was fun, especially when they'd wink at me and give me quarters.

Back then I never mouthed off because I knew it was hard for him raising two girls. I tried to get excited with him about sports, but I wasn't very good at it. Once we went to a hockey game but Daisy threw up after she ate a hot dog. We even tried fishing down by the river, except Daisy would scream over the worms and get tangled up in the line. He didn't have the patience for our outings. Under his breath he'd swear. But they were just words and I got used to them.

I don't remember us doing too much together except being together. Kids would talk about trips they'd be taking with their parents or going for rides in the country. We just stayed home. But that was fine for us. Soon I forgot about the robbery and stopped worrying that it would happen again. In a way I thought the whole thing was a blessing.

Then one night for dinner Dad made us noodles with green specks in them. Daisy never liked her food to touch and she especially didn't like it all mixed up. But once in a while he'd try something new.

At first, Daisy tried to scrape the flecks away with her fork but they wouldn't come off. Dad told her to cut it out, but she didn't listen. Instead she started to pinch out the spots with her fingers. Her hands got all gummy and when she picked up her fork, it slipped to the floor. He yelled "Eat it!" but she shook her head and said, "No." He reached over to her plate, grabbed it and flung it against the wall. The dish shattered, but the food stuck to the wall like a clump of dangling white worms and I laughed. "So you think this is funny!" he said. He snatched my plate and hurled it towards the sink. It cracked the kitchen window. He stood up, lifting the corners of the kitchen table. Glasses tipped and tumbled, spilling milk everywhere and silverware crashed to the floor. "Get out of here!" he roared.

We ran into the living room and that's when we heard it—"I'm leaving you kids," he said. "Tonight!"

Daisy started to cry and asked if he was going away again. I told her no, that he was just talking. But I said that to make her feel better.

Suddenly he kicked open the kitchen door and ripped towards us, red-faced. "Didn't I tell you to get out!" Daisy gasped for air and I froze, not sure what to do, where to go. He lunged at us and twisting both our arms, he threw us towards the stairs. "Go to your rooms!" he said.

I helped Daisy with her pajamas and told her everything would be all right in the morning. Then I went to my room and sat on the bed listening for sounds from downstairs. I couldn't hear anything so I crept into the hall. I still couldn't hear anything. Slowly I inched down, step by step, until the rush of running water became clear. I crouched down on a stair near the wall where he wouldn't be able to see, and listened to the clatter of dishes. After a while he came into the living room and turned on the TV. I slipped back to my room and before going to bed, I opened my window so I could hear if the car was being taken out of the garage. Then I got into bed and fell asleep.

In the middle of the night I woke up. Dad was in my bed with his arm around me. He told me how sorry he was for what happened earlier and that he loved me and he stroked my hair. I told him I loved him too. He stayed there for a long time, rubbing my leg and being close to me. I smelled beer on his breath. I fell back asleep and in the morning, he was gone.

The next day when I went downstairs, he and Daisy were talking and laughing. He kidded me about being a sleepy head and I sat down and had some toast. It was a spring morning. We finished breakfast, grabbed our lunches and headed out the door. He kissed Daisy and she skipped out in front of me. He then told me he acted silly the night before. I said it was okay.

As I left the kitchen, he slid his hand from my waist to my backside and gave me a pat. I turned around and looked at him—he had never done that before. He smiled. I waved good-bye.

After that things changed between us. He would come to my room every so often and lie down beside me. It was usually after I was already asleep. When I was too young to realize, he made funny noises and would rock in the bed. It didn't bother me all that much, I suppose. Besides anything was better than to have him leave us.

Now when I think back to when it started, it was more like a dream than anything else.

🍁   🍁   🍁

Author's note:

This is the first published story I wrote. It was extrapolated from a longer work.

What makes a father sexually abuse his daughter? As a Child Protective worker, I learned there are often certain markers present: absence of the mother, placement of the child in an adult role, drug/alcohol abuse by the perpetrator.

What makes a daughter comply? Tragically, to feel safe and loved.

"A Father's Love" was first published by The Haworth Press.

Aunt Leona

"Peculiar," Auntie would say, when sniffing the raw chicken or describing Lillian from next door, who never left the house. It was her favorite word, her lexicon; not a term of derision she would emphatically explain, simply a statement of fact. And there were other words like "conundrum" and "vociferous" and "abstruse".

She hadn't been an English teacher as you might have expected. Retired English teachers have that way about them, that general, non-specific, disapproving way. Not Aunt Leona. Neither teaching, nor children were her remotest concern, (myself excluded).

Auntie had been an executive secretary, a graduate of the "prestigious" Barnes Business School. She typed ninety words a minute and could transcribe any conversation in curious hieroglyphic curls and lines. I knew this for a fact, since I would occasionally visit Aunt Leona at her "position".

Dressed in my latest Sunday outfit, with matching hat and patent-leather shoes, I'd be taken downtown in Father's Buick and let off at the revolving doors on Washington Street. The Ellicott Square Building, where Leona worked, engulfed a city block. Marble walls, geometric inlaid floors, and rich dark wood welcomed me inside where, in my cleated shoes, I tap-danced to the elevators. Back then, the operators wore white gloves. "Fourth floor, please," I'd say. Moments later I'd stroll primly down the center of the corridor, carefully assessing each mahogany door, looking for the familiar, frosted-glass panel that read, Mr. Vincent Tucker, Esq., and in the lower right-hand corner, Miss Leona Drajem, Sec. I'd then enter, turning the chunky brass knob.

Auntie would be perched behind a huge wooden desk, in a blue suit with a scalloped collar and a crisp white blouse. Sometimes she'd be typing, sitting up tall; other times, she'd be on the phone. Mr. Tucker sat in an office directly behind hers, and you could see him whenever the connecting door was open, which it usually was.

They had an easy relationship, having worked together for almost thirty-five years. She made coffee, arranged for his dry cleaning, and bought presents for his wife. Routine like a married couple, Father had said.

On some days, mostly Saturdays or special school holidays, Mr. Tucker's son, Howard who was three years older than I, would also come to the office, and after the grown-up work was finished, the four of us would go out, as Auntie would say, for "a fashionably-late, continental lunch." I'd order a Shirley Temple with a small paper umbrella and two maraschino cherries.

Mr. Tucker and Auntie were very formal with each other. She called him Mr. Tucker. And he'd say, "Miss Drajem, don't even think of having a salad, order the filet."

But that all so very long ago.

The minister's words now reverberated in the church. "Having remembered our dear Leona, let us all open our prayer books to page twenty-three..."

I readjusted myself in the pew, and mouthed the printed words along with the congregation, but my thoughts remained in the past.

How old had Leona been when Mr. Tucker died? Could she have been in her early fifties, the age I am now? How awful it must have been for her. Within a matter of weeks, her employer of decades came down with the flu and died. Suddenly, she was no longer the independent career woman with her own apartment and fine crepe wool suits.

It was cruel how she had been treated. Mr. Tucker's thriving law practice was sold to a cousin and, without notice, her position was irreverently filled by a much younger woman of "questionable qualifications" and, even more upsetting, "suspicious character".

For the following thirty years, she lived an uneventful life. No more need to take the bus downtown or work after hours. But losing her job and taking such an early retirement had taken its toll. While she had become an award-winning gardener, her carefree personality changed. And in her later years, she would fret about the oddest things, the overabundance of bacteria in food or water and the queerest obsession with hand washing.

Reverend Walters continued, "On behalf of Miss Drajem's family, I would like to thank all of you for taking the time on this glorious spring morning to pray for Leona. She will be remembered with love and affection." He nodded and, as the organist played a short Mozart piece, he escorted me to the back of the church.

At the end of the receiving line, a gray-haired man extended his hand and gave me a fierce shake. "Elizabeth, you don't remember me, do you?"

The man had an uncanny likeness to Mr. Tucker, short, slightly balding, and thick in the middle.

"I'm Howard Tucker, Vincent's boy."

"Howard, of course. How kind of you to come."

"Your aunt was a class act. I was so sorry to hear about her death. We all loved her."

"Thank you. And how is your mother?"

"Well, she passed five years ago."

"I'm so sorry. I'm afraid I didn't know."

"Really? In fact, that was the last time I saw Leona. She had come to mother's funeral."

"Now, I do feel foolish. Auntie never said a word to me."

"Don't give it another thought. Anyway I wanted to extend my condolences. And how is your father?"

"Father died earlier this year."

"Dear, my sincerest apologies. Now we are both orphans."

I smiled, understanding what he meant. Finding yourself without any parent did leave a hole in one's heart.

"So all these arrangements were left up to you?"

"Hardly. Aunt Leona was so organized, everything was planned and paid for years ago."

He reached for my hand again and squeezed with less force. "Leona was such a take-charge kind of gal. Ahead of her time in many ways, I suspect. She was a loyal employee to my father, so very kind to me, and a grand friend to my mother. May she rest in peace."

I thanked him for his thoughtfulness. He then squared his hat on his head and stepped into the midday sunshine.

On my way home, I reran the conversation of our brief encounter. Something he had said made me wonder. While Auntie had never spoken badly about Mrs. Tucker, "grand friends" seemed a bit of a stretch, especially since there had been rumors whispered at the kitchen table by my parents; rumors of a liaison of sorts between Auntie and Mr. Tucker that went beyond the office. But after Mr. Tucker died, still a married man, the assumptions and insinuations dissipated.

What did it matter now? After all, their lives had been lived.

Only a few last details needed to be handled. Auntie's estate had to be settled and her flat cleared.

At two o'clock the next day, I met with Henry Banks, Leona's lawyer. He was a tall, gangly man with very thick glasses.

"Elizabeth," he said, "your aunt's will stipulates that you are the sole beneficiary of her estate."

I nodded politely. This was hardly a shock. She had lived in Father's house for more than three decades, and the little she had would hardly be much.

He continued. "Besides her jewelry and bank account, there is a safe deposit box with some personal papers, as well as stock certificates."

"Stocks?"

"Yes, surely she told you about these."

"I'm afraid not."

He laughed. "You're kidding."

I felt uneasy. What was so funny?

"Your aunt was a very wealthy woman."

"Aunt Leona? She lived like a church mouse."

"I don't know how she lived. But she has holdings of more than two million dollars."

Shocked, my heart skipped a beat, not only by the amount of the money, but the secrecy of it. How could a person squirrel away so much without a soul knowing?

"But that's not possible. She hadn't worked since the sixties. Her employer died suddenly, and she had no retirement except for barest social security."

He shook his head. "Don't ask me. But you are one lucky lady."

I drove home in a daze. Where would Auntie have gotten so much money? From Mr. Tucker before he died? Did they have an affaire d'coeur after all? Had there been a life insurance policy? Did she quit because of it? But certainly Mrs. Tucker would have gotten that. And if Mrs. Tucker and Auntie were such grand friends…well, none of this made sense.

I went immediately to the bank and checked the safe deposit box. Stock certificates from AT&T, Chrysler, and even Microsoft filled the drawer to overflowing. Stocks issued, as late as the previous summer, were also in the pile. Maybe Auntie was ahead of her time, as Howard had suggested. But where had she gotten the seed money?

I unrolled each page, set it aside, and continued to rummage for whatever personal papers Mr. Banks had referred to.

The first thing I came across, buried under the stocks, was a note written on the softest pink stationery from Mrs. Tucker. *"We must help each other through this difficult time. Since neither of us will be able to keep our dearest Vincent to ourselves, we must let him go. Be strong, together we can do this. Enclosed is a token for your service."* Whatever monies or check that may have been enclosed, were, of course, long gone. Also tucked neatly inside the envelope, was a prayer card from Warren's Funeral Parlor. Mr. Tucker died on January 2nd of 1969. So Aunt Leona did appear to have received some severance pay. But how much could it possibly have been?

A folded bit of yellowed newspaper was wedged on the bottom of the drawer. I carefully unraveled it. It was a full-size picture page from the Buffalo Evening News, dated February 12, 1968, almost one year prior to Mr. Tucker's death.

Immediately, my attention focused on two people holding plaques. My eyes dropped to the caption. *Mr. Vincent Tucker, a prominent Buffalo Attorney, and Miss Lucinda Smythe, the owner of Smythe Employment Agency, each accepted The Citizen of the Year Award. Mr. Tucker was honored for his Pro Bono Project and Miss Smythe for her Boys' and Girls' Clubs Scholarship Fund. The event was held last evening at the Hotel Statler.*

Mr. Tucker, younger than I remembered him, was handsomely attired in a tuxedo. He smiled proudly for the camera. The woman, Lucinda Smythe, who stood next to him, was dressed less formally, in what looked to be, a pin-striped, two-piece suit that was fashionably short and sharply tailored. Her dark hair was cut in a straight wedge, giving her a remarkably modern look.

As I refolded the page, I wondered why this had been left with Auntie's valuable papers. Could this have been the last photograph that Auntie had of Mr. Tucker, or possibly, the most attractive?

Lastly, an old blue Buffalo Savings Bank book from 1967 lay in the farthest corner of the metal box. Carefully I ran my finger down the handwritten deposits. Leona had saved one hundred dollars regularly once per month, until 1969, after which time, her deposits had quadrupled. Given that 1969 was the year that Mr. Tucker died, and she had lost her job, this was most curious. Where had the money come from?

My eyes followed pages of entries that continued through the year 1978, with regular deposits and occasional withdrawals. The last page of the book had been stamped in red with the words *Closed Out*. Quickly I added the amounts in my head. Nine years at over five thousand per year totaled close to fifty thousand dollars. While a formidable sum for today, it was an exorbitant figure twenty years ago.

I stuffed the certificates back into the long drawer and took the rest of the contents home.

The following day, I decided to empty out Auntie's apartment. It was a task that I had considered handing over to a woman I knew who dealt with estates. But now with so many unanswered questions, I changed my mind. I couldn't let these loose ends haunt me, especially since I knew what I was looking for.

Auntie's desk in the living room was my first stop. She kept meticulous records. Electric, gas, telephone, water bills were arranged alphabetically, paper-clipped together, and angled into cubby holes. But these were of little interest. I was looking for bank account statements, either checking or savings. In the bottom double drawer, pale green statements from Forester Savings and Loan sat neatly stacked. I dug them out and began my search. Did one-hundred dollar weekly deposits continue to this day?

My eyes poured over the columns. As I continued down the pile, and as the years digressed, only her automatic social security deposits showed up—that was until 1997. Suddenly those weekly amounts resurfaced and remained constant back to 1978, when she had her other, earlier account.

I reclined in Auntie's old wooden swivel chair and tried to remember if anything of import had occurred in 1997. Five years ago, echoed in my mind. Then I recalled something Howard Tucker had said at the funeral—his mother had died five years ago. A shiver ran through me. Was it simply a coincidence that the money began with Mr. Tucker's death and ended with Mrs. Tucker's death? Did this money pass from Mrs. Tucker to Auntie?

My mind raced, as an unusual scenario toyed with my otherwise practical mind. Did Auntie know something? Was she blackmailing Mrs. Tucker? Had Mrs. Tucker done something to her husband? Something like murder?

This was madness of course, a middle-aged woman's ruminations and for a moment I thought of contacting the bank to see who deposited the money into Auntie's account. But did I really need to know? Then another unsettling thought occurred. Was an inheritance from blackmail still rightfully mine?

I tossed the statements back into the drawer and told myself that any further investigation would probably raise more questions than answers, especially since all the parties were now deceased. I had to get on with my life. I reached over and called my friend who dealt in estates and told her that I was interested in her services.

Before leaving, I went into Auntie's bedroom and collected her jewelry box, my last bit of inheritance. I stood and sighed heavily at the entrance to her bedroom, smelling her lingering Chanel #5. "Good night Auntie," I said. And for the first time since her death, I sobbed and rushed from the house.

Later that evening, I began to think of my own future. I put aside all the papers that I had collected in the past twenty-four hours and opened Auntie's jewelry box.

It was the string of natural pearls that I hoped to find, but what drew my attention was a pink envelope tucked inside the lid pocket. I took a deep breath, dislodged the flap, and read the contents.

> *June 10, 1997*
> *Dearest Leona,*
>   *I am ready to die but don't want to leave unfinished business. We live our lives from such egocentric perspectives that sometimes it is*

difficult to know or understand the truth. Anyway, I feel it necessary to unburden myself.

Since Vincent's death, I have known a certain truth that you could have only surmised—I never loved the man. And since I never loved him, I never hated him either. This, of course, was your cross to bear. My interest in taking care of the situation was simple—after forty years of my humiliating devotion, he owed me. I had not allowed him to divorce me for you, and I certainly was not about to permit an ending of our marriage so he could be with that tramp, Lucinda.

As I review our rather interesting relationship, I see how portentous our luncheon at Laube's was so very long ago. We were two women whose parallel lives intersected. We were honorable women who kept our promise and secret. Enclosed is my final token of gratitude. Love, Rita.

What was this about? Certainly not a case of blackmail on Leona's part. Mrs. Tucker had given her money freely to Auntie. Was guilt the underlying reason? Had Mrs. Tucker killed her husband and was the money restitution for Auntie, the grieving mistress? I breathed a sigh of relief. While a murder may have been committed, I felt consoled that my new found wealth was not based on an ill-gotten gain, at least on Auntie's part.

I gathered the papers to dispose of them properly. It was truly time to let things go. But suddenly the note that I had found in the safe deposit box with the funeral card, snagged my attention. On the corner of the page, a date was written. It wasn't January of 1969, the month of Mr. Tucker's untimely demise, but three month's prior, October 12, 1968.

I reread the note, but this time from a new perspective:

It was then that I realized "this difficult time" was in reference to events before his death; and "we must let him go" was a decision made; and "together we can do this." was a plan, pre-meditated; and "a token for your service", was payment for a job rendered.

My stomach lurched as a clear, distinct understanding flooded my consciousness. Suddenly, one of Auntie's words came to mind. "Collusion."

      🍁   🍁   🍁

Author's note:

This story, told by a narrator, is about people who have died. They leave behind footprints, photographs, letters, knitted cozies for toasters. They also leave behind a personal history often never discovered.

We tend to reminisce about the past with rose-colored glasses. We tend to think past lives were vastly uncomplicated from our own. But human nature's wants and needs never change. And a jilted lover from any time, present or past, remains thematic, and, thankfully for writers, never goes out of style.

A Hero Among Us

As retirement approached, Walden Belmont faced an uncertain future, not that it was unwelcomed but he had learned from the past—things never got better, just worse.

Walden worked as a civil servant in the city's Assessment Department. It was torment each day, each year, like a case of terminal cancer that never ended. It was the triteness, Walden supposed, that made it so unbearable. The petty quarrels, the demanding public, his fellow employees who bemoaned their children, their marriages, and their unfathomable illnesses. It was also the sameness, the wearisome sweep of the second hand that made five minutes seem like a lifetime.

To escape the tedium and make the days tolerable, Walden drank, at times to oblivion. But as the years passed, the anesthetic effect lost its punch, leaving him to deal with events in a brutally sober manner. The only thing that made him smile was watching talking animals in commercials, dogs especially.

With retirement nipping at his heels, a thorny decision loomed—What the heck was he going to do?

His options? Well, he could procure a permanent stool at his local watering hole as early as eleven in the morning, or he could watch TV until 6 AM and sleep until it was dark again. But neither grabbed his interest and shortly before his dreaded retirement party, he considered one final possibility—suicide, preferably painless, definitely irrevocable.

Again he considered the choices. There were two, shotgun to the head or carbon monoxide in a closed garage. He leaned toward the latter. It wasn't bloody and since most people who died this way were often found in a couch potato position it couldn't be all that traumatic. The problem was he'd have to get a car and a garage. Such needless expense. Blowing his brains out held a distant appeal. First, it was manly. Second, it didn't involve any investment since he already had a rifle and ammo. But it was messy and, unless he did it somewhere other than his room, the clean up would be an imposition, for which his landlady would hound him to Hades.

While spending an inordinate amount of time considering these matters, the days crept forward as did his retirement gala. He didn't want a party, who would? But when he said no, he was told that they would simply throw him a surprise party. He sickened at the thought and conceded that it was better to opt for a planned event than any that suggested unpreparedness or ambush.

He wore an old suit that fit poorly, short in the legs, unable to be buttoned. What did it matter? His underwear was clean and he showered.

The event was held in a Polish restaurant within walking distance of his rented room. As he plodded across the two block area, he made some quick calculations. A few drinks, a buffet meal, and his mono-syllabic acceptance speech for the plaque that was routinely given, certainly couldn't last more than two hours. When he entered the restaurant, he checked his watch, 7:30. By 9:30, he'd be home just in time for Frasier.

Once he got inside, the first thing that struck him was the dense crowd. He looked around for someone he recognized and only noticed, Jenny, his secretary standing alone in a distant corner. Suddenly, out of nowhere, Louis Pelter, a guy he had worked with years prior jumped out at him. "Hey, Wally. How ya doin'?" and he pounded Walden's back.

Walden wavered to keep his equilibrium. "Louie, what are you doing here?"

"It's your retirement party. I'm here to pay my respects and return the loan. Let me get you a drink."

Walden nodded as other vaguely familiar people rallied around him. "Yo, Wal." "Congratulations, Wal." "Wuz up? Wal."

He looked into the crowd. Who were all these people?

A man pulled him by his arm. It was Bill Safer, his desk partner, who had retired two years previous. "Wal, it's great seeing you. Is this a party or what? Biggest one, I've ever been to. Man, your take's going to be major. Oh, by the way, this is my son, Robie. You remember, you bailed him out of jail."

Robie came forward, a tall young man with his hand out.

Walden shook it. "How you doing Robie?"

Before Robie answered, a middle-aged woman rushed over.

"You probably don't remember me, I'm Larry Woodman's wife. I never thanked you for all your help."

Walden recalled Larry's long days in the hospital and the endless cups of coffee they shared. "He was a brave man," Walden said.

And so the evening went on. The throng of people were not only employees past and present, but their family members he never met.

Suddenly, a band began to play "For He's a Jolly Good Fellow", and the mob joined in.

There was no plaque for Walden. Instead, he was presented with a discrete envelope and a large gift-wrapped picture. "Open it" the crowd yelled. He ripped away the paper and laughed long and hard. It was a painting of four dogs playing poker.

That evening, Walden missed Frasier. The next day, he got rid of the bullets and thanked whoever was listening that he never wasted money on a car.

🍁   🍁   🍁

Author's note:

September 11th, an event burned into our collective memory, was the initial flicker for "A Hero". The tragic and awe-inspiring stories of selfless heroism by everyday people was, is, and will always be, a celebration of humanity.

"A Hero" is also about the inner and outer person, the composite of who we are, in both predilection and contradiction.

Lastly, "A Hero" is about saying "Thank you".

0-595-27183-9